The Duke of Darkness
A Legend To Love

Cora Lee

ISBN 9781944477103

More Than Words Press
PO Box 480 042
New Haven, MI 48048

http://coraleeauthor.wordpress.com/more-than-words-press/

Cover by Teresa Sprecklemeyer, Midnight Muse Designs

Editing by Jude Simms.

Special thanks to Miranda Bly, Karen Simpson, Lori Farner Dykes, Heather Cuva, Regina Thewise, Peggy Collins, Frankie Reviews, and Roxane Twisdale for help with Rhuddlan's name.

Men's evil manners live in brass; their virtues we write in water.

—William Shakespeare, *Henry VIII*

Chapter One

North Wales
September 1819

Thump

THE DUKE OF RHUDDLAN'S hand flew to the back of his head as he pitched forward over the neck of his horse. Stars exploded before his eyes and pain spread through his skull, while sticky warmth began to ooze through his fingers. He managed to sling an arm around the horse's neck to keep himself from falling off, but only just. The sudden clinch made the poor beast panic and it started thrashing about, determined to dislodge Rhuddlan. The tighter he held on, the harder the horse bucked, until it succeeded in dumping its ducal rider onto the muddy road.

Rhuddlan landed on his side, his head bouncing mercifully off his arm—flung up at the last moment to shield his face from the impact—rather than the ground. He lay there for a moment or two with his eyes closed, trying to clear his mind and take stock of his body.

But when he opened his eyes, he saw only darkness.

He held a hand up to his face, close enough for him to smell the damp earth on his fingers, but his eyes registered nothing. Rolling onto his back, he spread his arms out wide and shut his eyes again, hoping that the next time he opened them his vision would be restored.

It wasn't.

"Your Grace!" a voice called from somewhere far away. "Your Grace, are you hurt?"

He struggled to sit up, loath to appear weak before a stranger. But a great wave of dizziness washed over him and knocked him back to the ground.

Fabric swished in his ear as if someone in a gown or long robe had knelt down beside him. A cool, calloused hand smoothed his brow, stroked his cheek. The blackness began to fade when he opened his eyes once more, but it was replaced by a world twirling like a demented ballerina and he shut them tight again.

"Your Grace, don't move for a moment. You've had a nasty fall."

The voice was feminine, English, and he heard its owner suck in a breath when her fingers met the blood oozing from his wound.

"I assure you, madam, that I—"

"I beg your pardon, Your Grace," the voice interrupted, "but if you're about to tell me you're perfectly well, then you can save your breath. I can see very well what kind of state you're in."

Her tone was brusque but polite and Rhuddlan's world was still spinning, so he held his piece. He was clearly in need of assistance, and if this girl had plans to finish him off she'd have done so by now.

"Very well," he murmured, heartened that his words were properly enunciated, not slurred and sloppy like his thoughts. "What do you suggest?"

He heard a second figure join the first, kneeling on the road beside him. "First, we stop the bleeding, Your Grace. Can you sit up if we help you?"

Another woman, older by the sound of her voice and Welsh. Rhuddlan started to nod, then thought better of it. "I believe so."

Two arms slid across his back and slowly levered him into a sitting position, holding him there as someone pressed a cloth to the base of his skull.

"How bad is it?" he asked, hoping the women didn't hear the apprehension in his voice.

They were both silent for a long moment before the younger one spoke. "It's messy."

"Head wounds do tend to bleed a lot," he returned slowly. He'd certainly seen enough of them on the battle field to know.

"Do you know what happened, Your Grace?"

He pressed his lips together. It could have been a random attack. God knew Rhuddlan tried to take care of the people who depended on him, but not everyone appreciated his methods. Yet he was nearly certain his brother Nick was behind this, quite possibly the Duke of Cumberland, too. The pair of them had been thick as thieves for the past three years, united in a single purpose: to remove Rhuddlan from power and gain control of the dukedom's finances.

But Rhuddlan said none of that aloud. "I didn't see who it was," he answered instead, which was true enough. "I didn't even see what was thrown."

"We should get you out of the road, Your Grace," the older woman said. "Do you think you can walk?"

He opened his eyes, keeping them cast downward toward the dirt. The road was still spinning, but not as fast as it had been. He cautiously lifted his lids and tried to focus on the women assisting him, but the effort—and the glaring sun—only nauseated him. "Slowly, perhaps."

They got him to his feet and helped him shuffle from the road to a nearby cottage, while a black blur that might have been a dog led the way. The distance must only have been a dozen yards or so but they seemed to take hours to cover it, and Rhuddlan was exhausted when at last they set him in a hard wooden chair. The older woman disappeared with a glance at her associate that he couldn't quite make out.

"Mrs. Davies will fetch a physician, Your Grace, and see to your horse."

Rhuddlan twisted around trying to look at the younger woman as she stood behind him, but she turned his head back and bent it slightly forward.

"You must be the healer, then," he said.

"The healer?"

He felt a cloth once again pressed against his wound and suppressed a grunt of pain. "I assume that's why you stayed with me while..."

"Mrs. Davies," she supplied.

"...while Mrs. Davies finds my physician and horse."

"Mrs. Davies is better with horses than I am. It takes no great skill to hold a cloth to a wound."

He'd been left in the care of a girl devoid of competence? He propped his elbows on his thighs and dropped his face into his hands. "Who are you, then, if not a healer?"

"Miss Stone, Your Grace. I mostly make my living with a needle and thread."

At least he'd have someone to sew up his scalp if the physician failed to appear. "You live here with Mrs. Davies?"

"I live here. She lives next door."

This stretch of land was part of the Rhuddlan estate—small farms and cottages with kitchen gardens leased to families that couldn't afford to purchase property of their own. "My tenants, then."

"Yes, Your Grace."

"Have you ever met my brother?"

"Which one?"

Rhuddlan pressed the heels of his hands into his eyes. His elder brother—the one who should have inherited the dukedom—had been killed fighting at the Battle of New Orleans four years ago. Rhuddlan didn't think of him as often as he used to, but the memories still hurt when they surfaced.

"Lord Nicholas," he answered tightly. Thoughts of his younger brother were painful, too.

"I haven't had the pleasure."

She said it with no great enthusiasm in her voice, yet no hostility either. He supposed she could have been lying, but came back to the realization that if she'd wanted him dead or incapacitated she could easily have seen to it by now.

"Perhaps you should lie down, Your Grace. My bed is just through that door—"

He wanted to protest, but between the dizziness and pain he couldn't bring himself to react with anything except relief. "Yes, thank you."

She took one of his hands and clamped it to the back of his head, holding the cloth in place, then slipped one arm around his waist and hoisted him to his feet. She was several inches shorter than he and Rhuddlan wasn't sure how she managed to keep him from crashing to the floor, but he was delivered safely to a narrow bed and sank down onto it, taking extra care to lie on his side.

The next hour was a blur of misery. His wound eventually ceased bleeding, and the cottage finally stopped spinning long enough for Rhuddlan to take in his surroundings. But the nausea refused to retreat, nor could the physician seem to banish the feeling when he arrived. The man set his case on what looked to be a crude dressing table, pushing a plain wooden hairbrush and some faded ribbons aside to make room for his phials, but the concoction he mixed up was as foul tasting as it was useless.

Rhuddlan dismissed the man, and carefully laid back down on the surprisingly soft sheets until Miss Stone roused him an indeterminate time later. By then the scent of his own blood had overpowered the smell of mint that seemed to be infused into the sheets, and he was ready to return to his own home.

"Your carriage is here, Your Grace," she said softly, laying a hand on his shoulder. "The coachman has brought a stable lad with him to see to your horse, as well."

"Good. Thank you." He allowed her to help him sit up, then to stand. "I will not forget the kindness you've shown to me today."

Her gaze drifted to the floor. "I only did what any decent person would do."

"Nevertheless," he replied, watching a few loose strands of blonde hair slide across her cheek. For a brief moment, he wondered if her hair was as soft as it looked or if his vision was still distorted. "I will remember it."

The coachman came in at that moment, and took over the support of Rhuddlan from Miss Stone, loading him into the carriage for the short drive back to Rhuddlan Hall. His head had cleared a little more by the time he arrived at the front door, and his principal secretary, Ian Vaughn, who appeared moments after the footman shut the big front door behind his master, was barely spinning at all.

"Your Grace." Vaughn dipped his head in a short bow. "Would you allow me to assist you—"

"I can walk on my own," Rhuddlan replied. His voice sounded gruff, but after nearly ten years in service to Rhuddlan, Vaughn was no doubt used to his employer's moods. "Come along, we have much to discuss."

Once the door of the study was closed, Rhuddlan made for the green velvet sofa and lowered himself upon it, motioning to Vaughn to close the heavy curtains that framed each window. He wasn't about to lie down in the presence of another person, particularly a subordinate, but the soft cushions would be more comfortable for his aching body than the stiff oak chair at his desk, and the darkness helped relieve the discomfort of the harsh sunlight.

"Where would you like to start, Your Grace?" Vaughn asked, settling himself at his own, smaller desk covered in stacks of books and papers. "With the incident this afternoon?"

"What do you know about it?"

Vaughn cleared his throat. "I spoke to Mrs. Davies when she came here. She told me that you'd been injured, but didn't know the particulars."

"A blow to the back of the head," Rhuddlan clarified.

"You think it was Lord Nicholas?"

Rhuddlan closed his eyes briefly, fighting a wave of nausea when he opened them again. "It could have been random."

Vaughn frowned, glancing at his shoes before meeting his employer's eyes again. "It could have been anyone, Your Grace. But given your brother's hostility toward you, and the encouragement he receives from the Duke of Cumberland..."

Rhuddlan sighed, more heavily than he'd intended. Nick was nearly nine years younger than he was, and had been his constant companion when they were boys despite the difference in their ages. They'd drifted apart a bit as they grew older, further still when Rhuddlan and their oldest brother purchased commissions in the Royal Army and marched away to fight in Britain's wars. When their father died and Rhuddlan inherited the dukedom, Nick had turned to Prince Ernest Augustus, the Duke of Cumberland and the King's fifth son, to fill the void.

"Cumberland, yes." The complete opposite of Rhuddlan, who no doubt promised Nick power and wealth that his own brother wouldn't give him. "Any sightings of him?"

"No, Your Grace. As far as anyone knows, he's still in Hanover."

"That's good, at least." Not that a little thing like distance would stop him—or Nick, for that matter—but it was something. "Have there been other incidents today?"

Vaughn shook his head. "Nothing since the mill fire."

Rhuddlan turned slightly sideways and rested his temple against the back of the sofa, inhaling the scent of the leather-bound books on the shelves behind him. A fire had been deliberately set three days ago in a grain mill on another part of the estate. It had happened in the middle of the night and no one had been hurt, but every person employed there was now looking for a new way to provide for their families.

"And no proof who set the fire?" He knew very well there wasn't, but he couldn't help asking.

"No, Your Grace," Vaughn repeated. "Though the food baskets were delivered today. The next set will be delivered a week hence."

That made Rhuddlan's mind a little more easy. At least his people would eat. "Good. I have another task to add to your list—find out everything you can about a woman named Stone who lives in one of the thatched cottages near the road to the village. And discover what you can about Mrs. Davies, as well. She is Miss Stone's next door neighbor."

Vaughn scribbled across a piece of paper on his desk. "Do you think they had anything to do with your attack?"

Did he? Rhuddlan shook his head, then winced as the pain overtook him. "No," he answered, closing his eyes tightly. "I doubt they would have helped me if they were the ones who caused me harm in the first place." It was more likely that at least one of them would come begging a favor of him, and he wanted to be prepared. "But I need to be sure."

"I will see to it, Your Grace."

"Good." Another weight lifted, at least for the time being. "What else have I missed today?"

"What a mess he made of your sheets," Mrs. Davies lamented, running a hand over a section of embroidery that hadn't been bloodied.

Olivia Stone suppressed a sigh. She'd worked for weeks on the pillowcases alone, pillowcases that were now covered in patchy stains from the Duke of Rhuddlan's head wound. "They may yet come clean," she replied, though even she could hear the lack of conviction in her voice.

"Certainly, and I may yet become a duchess," Mrs. Davies said with a wink. Then she sobered, asking quietly, "Do you have another set, my dear?"

Olivia pictured the soft linen she'd purchased last week, already sewn into sheets and decorated with carefully stitched honeysuckle vining along some of the edges. She'd saved for months to buy that material, planning to make the sheets a Christmas gift for neighbors.

And they were the only other sheets she possessed.

But Olivia didn't want Mrs. D. to worry—she did enough of that on Olivia's behalf as it was. "I do, yes."

"Good. You'll be over for supper tonight, won't you?"

Another reason for the Christmas gift: if not for Mrs. D. issuing her almost nightly invitation to dine with her and her live-in companion, Miss Hatch, Olivia would likely go to bed hungry more often than not. She earned money each month taking in sewing to provide for herself and her big black dog—curled up contentedly by the front door—but too many of her customers had begun patronizing the new dressmaker's shop in the village, and her income had steadily been declining. The generosity of her neighbors lessened the strain on her tight budget, and giving them good quality linen with Olivia's own embroidery was a way of saying thank you.

"I will, just as soon as I get these stains soaking in some cold water."

She bid Mrs. D. farewell and grabbed two buckets, heading toward the small stream that flowed a quarter mile behind her cottage. The water in it was always cold as melted snow, and it might be enough to get the blood out of her sheets.

Olivia was halfway home again with her buckets filled nearly to the brim when a shadow fell across her path. She sucked in a breath and held it, recognizing the smell of his expensive cologne before her eyes reached his face.

Sir George Grayson. He claimed to have been courting her for the past several months, except his addresses were anything but courtly...and even less welcome. He treated her more like prey than a potential wife, despite his professed love for her. Olivia knew it was her connections he loved, though, not her. If not for her relation to Viscount Teverton—never mind how distant it was—Sir George wouldn't have given her a second thought.

Too bad he also knew her real identity, and wasn't above blackmailing her with it.

"Aren't you going to greet me?" He came to a halt directly in front of her, a box held in one hand while the other reached for her.

She set down one of the heavy buckets and offered him her hand, trying, as usual, to disguise her reluctance. If he detected anything but willing obedience in her voice or manner, there was no telling what he'd do. "Good afternoon, Sir George."

He took her hand, giving it a hard squeeze. "Good afternoon to you, Olivia. What's the water for?"

She couldn't let him know that there had been another man in her home, but if he caught her lying to him... She shuddered internally and pushed the thought away. "Some of my linens were stained, and I need to soak them before the stain sets."

He yanked her closer to him, sloshing water onto her shoes from the bucket she still held. "Linen? As in bed sheets?"

She swallowed hard and dropped her gaze, her whole body tensing. "Yes. But it's not what you think."

"It's not what I think? What do you know about what I think?"

It was a trick question, of course. It always was. "I didn't mean to presume, Sir George."

His grip on her hand relaxed a little. He liked her best when he thought she was meek and biddable. "I'm sure you didn't. Tell me, then—what happened to your sheets?"

Olivia slid her hand gently from his, slowly setting down the other bucket of water in case she needed to run. He'd never seriously harmed her—he seemed to enjoy her fear more than her pain—but he'd threatened to do so more times than she cared to recall.

"Th-there's blood on them," she replied quietly, clasping her hands together at her waist. Perhaps this time she could quell the shaking before he noticed it.

"Blood on your sheets?" His tone was even, almost conversational. But his eyes had narrowed and his cheeks had flushed. "Who were you tupping, you little whore?"

"No, Sir George, that isn't what ha—"

"And now you lie to me about it?" He took a step closer to her, grabbing the neckline of her dress in one big fist. "What have I told you about lying to me?"

Olivia fought to control her breathing. The more panic she displayed, the longer he would torture her. "That there would be consequences," she said as steadily as she could. Part of her badly wanted to explain the situation, to exonerate herself of the wrongdoing he was imagining. But she knew that would only anger him more, so she clamped her mouth shut.

"That's right. Would you like to tell me the truth now, or do you want to find out what those consequences are?"

His words were harsh, almost a whisper, but they frightened her more than if he'd been shouting. "I am telling you the truth," she managed, fighting tears. She'd only cried in front of him once and he'd stomped away in disgust, but she couldn't be sure he'd react that way a second time. What if her tears enraged him even more?

"Perhaps I should burn down your little house, hm? With no place to live, you'd have to marry me...or freeze to death this winter." She clenched her teeth together hard to keep from responding, but he smiled. "While I'm at it, I'll put your neighbors' hovel to the torch, too. That would teach you not to lie to me, wouldn't it?"

Faint but persistent barking filtered through the air, simultaneously filling her with hope and dread, her heart racing as the sound grew louder. What would George do to the animal who came upon them? To a person accompanying the animal?

His eyes stayed focused on hers for a moment that felt like years. Then he slowly released her gown and opened the box he'd been carrying. Her eyes widened as he drew out an ivory-handled pistol and touched the tip of the barrel to her chest.

"Don't make a sound."

She nodded slowly, barely breathing as he turned and fired in the direction of the barking. Peering around his shoulder, Olivia could see her dog, Artie, loping down the hill toward them. He started when the gun fired and she pressed her hands to her mouth to stifle the scream that tore from her throat.

Artie laid his ears back and snarled, racing toward Sir George and the sound of the shot. Sir George pulled a second pistol from the box and took aim, sending the tears pouring down Olivia's face.

She gathered every ounce of courage she had and shouted, *"Loup! Arrête-toi!"* He didn't always listen when he thought she was in danger, but he'd been a herding dog before the late Mr. Davies had brought him home from Waterloo and still reflexively responded to commands given in French. Thankfully, he stopped in his tracks and dropped into a low crouch. Mrs. Davies' form crested the hill a second later and Sir George lowered his weapon, concealing it behind his back, as the smell of gunpowder hung thick in the air.

"Olivia? Are you down there?" Mrs. D. called. "I forgot to ask you—"

"I'll be right there," she called in a shaky voice, defying Sir George's order for silence once again, hoping he'd leave Mrs. D. alone if she stayed far enough away. To him, she murmured, "If I don't go up there, she'll come down here."

Sir George gave her one final glare, then jerked his chin in Mrs. D.'s direction. Olivia lifted her buckets of water and tried to walk normally, whistling to Artie to follow her up the hill. Mrs. D. held out an arm and Olivia passed her one of the buckets, threading her free arm through Mrs. D.'s, hoping to draw strength from the older woman.

"Just a few more minutes and you'll be safe," Mrs. D. whispered.

Olivia spent her remaining energy maintaining a calm countenance and a regular stride all the way back to Mrs. D.'s cottage. Once she rounded the corner into the little kitchen garden, she let go. Dropping her bucket and leaning against the stone wall of the house, Olivia covered her face and cried out her terror, her anger, her relief that no one had been hurt today. Mrs. D. hugged her, let Olivia cry on her shoulder as Artie leaned against her legs.

"How bad was it this time?" Mrs. D. asked when Olivia had cried herself out.

"You heard the shot?" It was all Olivia could bring herself to say, but it was enough to convey the danger they'd been in. Sir George had described his pistols in detail over the last few weeks, including the animals he'd killed with them.

Mrs. D. hugged Olivia to her again. "You poor girl."

"I can't live like this anymore," Olivia choked out. "What am I going to do?"

Mrs. D. rubbed Olivia's back in slow circles, and Olivia let the motion and the gentle breeze calm her, let them carry away thoughts of what could have happened at the base of the hill. When she'd cried her last, she lifted her face and wiped her eyes, bending down to give Artie his own hug and kiss. "You're a good boy, Loup Garou."

"You do have one option."

Olivia straightened, keeping one hand on Artie's furry head as she faced Mrs. D. "Teverton?"

Mrs. D. didn't react to the name, but she didn't have to. It was a discussion they'd had before. Lord Teverton was Olivia's closest living relative and head of her family, but the only thing she knew about him was that he owned an estate near Liverpool.

"What if he turns me away?"

No one could legally force Olivia to marry Sir George, but if she went to Teverton for help and he refused, her only choice would be between Sir George and slow starvation as the demand for her work continued to decline and her past slowly caught up with her.

"But what if he doesn't?"

Olivia pressed the heels of her hands to her eyes. What if Teverton was an honorable man who promised to protect her? Did she even have paper to write him a letter and ask?

"What about His Grace?" she said suddenly, dropping her hands to her sides. The breeze picked up, carrying with it the scent of the mint growing a few feet away.

Mrs. D. took a step back. "What about him?"

"Well...he's here. Teverton is all the way in Liverpool. Or at a different estate completely. And the duke ought to be amenable to my situation—if I am hale and hearty, I can continue paying my rent every quarter."

Mrs. D. shook her head faintly. "You can't mean to ask him for help."

"At least I've made his acquaintance," Olivia replied slowly. "Better the devil you know."

"Devil is right," Mrs. D. said, her mouth pulling into a pucker as if she'd eaten something sour. "I know we helped him this afternoon, but that was basic decency. You know what they say about the man."

Olivia did know. She'd borrowed a battered copy of a story called *The Vampyre* from a friend in the village the previous week, and had read it aloud to Mrs. D. and Miss H. after dinner one evening. The two older ladies had exchanged a knowing look, and it had taken some doing to get Miss Hatch to elaborate.

"The Duke of Rhuddlan," she'd said with a shudder. "Some think he's like that. A vampire."

She'd refused to speak of it further, and Olivia had let it drop. But she'd made an inquiry or two when she returned the book a few days later, and Miss Hatch wasn't the only person who thought there was something unholy about His Grace.

Olivia frowned at Mrs. D., recalling the fraught conversation they'd had about Olivia's past when Sir George had first come calling. "Does that mean you believe the rumors about me?"

Her neighbor made a little gasping noise. "Of course not! I would never—"

"Then perhaps the rumors about him are equally as malicious."

Mrs. D. stood staring for several moments, but eventually nodded. "Perhaps."

Olivia felt Artie's fur slide through her fingers as he bolted away after a rabbit. "Then I'll make an appointment to see His Grace."

She felt calm for the first time in months, despite Mrs. D.'s disapproval. Nothing in her life had immediately changed, but at least she had a feasible plan. If the Duke of Rhuddlan tossed her out on her ear she'd be right back where she started, but she tamped that fear down. One thing at a time. And now she had something she could *do*.

Chapter Two

"YOUR WOUND IS healing well, Your Grace," the surgeon pronounced, straightening up and wiping his hands on a towel.

Rhuddlan grunted and rose from the chair he'd been sitting in. His head wound ought to be healing properly after applying alcohol to it nightly for nearly a week—a trick he discovered when he accidentally spilled whisky on a soldier's lacerated hand after Vimeiro, and noted how much faster it had healed than other similar wounds.

But his head was still tender and the surgeon's probing caused it to throb. "Good," he managed in tight voice.

"I'll return in two or three days to remove those stitches," the surgeon continued.

"No need," Rhuddlan countered. "My valet can do it." Harding had never so much as nicked his master with the shaving razor in eight years of service. He could certainly handle the snipping of a few threads.

"As you wish, Your Grace."

The surgeon collected his things and left, nearly colliding with Vaughn as the latter entered Rhuddlan's study.

"Your Grace, there's a woman here to see you," Vaughn said when the surgeon had shut the door behind him.

Rhuddlan mechanically passed a hand through his hair and returned to his seat behind the big desk. "What does she want?"

"She'd only say that it was important and would only take a moment of your time."

Of course she did—every petitioner did. Sometimes they actually did have important matters that were settled quickly, but more often they brought him issues of little significance and took up too much of his time. But they were his people, and it was his duty to see to them.

"*Who* is she, then?"

"Miss Stone, Your Grace." Rhuddlan must have given his secretary a puzzled look because Vaughn added, "The Miss Stone who tended you in her home when you were injured last week."

"Of course," Rhuddlan replied with a nod, linking the name with the face once again. "Your summary of the investigator's report was good."

"Thank you," the secretary returned with a small smile. "The full report is there on your desk."

"Good." Vaughn would have noted anything of interest in his summary, but information was always better when it came straight from the source. He ruffled the dark hair near his wound and sat back in his chair. "I'll see Miss Stone now."

Vaughn disappeared and returned a minute later with a plump blonde female in a rather plain pink dress. Her skin was pale, and she walked hesitantly behind the secretary, nearly bumping into him when he came to a halt before Rhuddlan's desk.

"Miss Stone, Your Grace."

Vaughn bowed and left, not needing to be told to get back to work. Miss Stone curtseyed deeply, and Rhuddlan could see her hands trembling as they clung to her skirt.

"Miss Stone...who helped me when I was struck in the head."

"Yes, Your Grace." Her voice was soft, almost timid as she straightened, as if she were facing down an angry father in the wake of some misdeed.

Was she afraid of him? Members of the peerage were wont to liken him to the devil, particularly after the incident with his cousin a few years back. Had the rumors filtered down to the lower classes?

"I did not thank you properly for your care of me that day," he replied with genuine gratitude. Vaughn's summary of the investigation had indicated that, not only had she and her neighbor come to Rhuddlan's rescue, but they had not told a soul about it afterwards. "If not for you, I would have been at the mercy of whomever happened by. And not everyone would have been as kind."

She flinched at his pronouncement, as if he'd raised his hand against her. "Miss Stone, are you well?"

"I–I have come to seek your protection."

"Protection from what?"

"Not what, who," she returned cautiously. "Sir George Grayson attempted to begin a courtship with me some months ago—"

"You should be flattered," Rhuddlan interjected, wondering if she wanted him to settle some lovers' spat. "Marriage to a knight would raise your standing considerably."

"But the attention is unwanted, Your Grace, and Sir George has become dangerous."

He watched her clasp her hands together, first in front of her then behind her back. Rhuddlan had never met Grayson, but had heard of him, and the memory returned to him now. There'd been a rumor circulating through the gaming hells in Town that Grayson had beaten a man senseless when a debt was repaid too slowly.

If he had nearly killed a man who was honorably repaying a debt, what would he do to a penniless female?

"Dangerous in what way?"

She took a deep breath in and held it for a moment before letting it out slowly. "He comes to my home uninvited, proclaiming that he'll kill any man who speaks to me...including Mr. Price down the road, who is happily married and old enough to be my grandfather." She paused and took another breath. "He has also threatened my next door neighbors—he says he'll burn down their home to punish me." Pause. Breath. "He tells me at least once during each visit how he'd like to disembowel my dog because 'the beast' tries to keep him away from me." Pause. Breath. "And his favorite subject is to tell me how, if I ever show interest in another man, he'll take me by surprise one day and shoot me in the head."

Her whole body was shaking by the time she finished, despite the pauses for what he assumed were calming breaths, and her gaze had drifted downward to the thick carpet at her feet. The fear wasn't for

Rhuddlan, then, but for Sir George Grayson. Was it real? Was she genuinely frightened or a superb actress?

"This is why you're asking for protection."

She hesitated, then answered haltingly, "Y-yes, Your Grace. The only family I have left is a distant cousin who lives near Liverpool, whom I've never met. I don't know if he would take me in or insist I give in and marry Sir George despite his threats."

Rhuddlan propped his elbows on his desk again and clasped his hands together. "And if George Grayson has his way, someone will be dead before you can get a letter to Liverpool."

"That is what I'm afraid of, yes."

Rhuddlan pressed his lips together. If she were acting, he would soon find out. And he'd make sure that she never attempted to take advantage of him again. But if she was in real danger, she needed immediate assistance. "Then you were right to come to me. You are my dependent and I will see to your safety."

The breath *whoosh*ed out of her. "Thank you, Your Grace."

"You so generously took me in when I was in need," he added, "it's only right that I repay the favor. Have you a maid or companion?"

Her posture had relaxed, but it stiffened again. "Only my dog."

"What about these neighbors that George is hell-bent on harming?"

"Mrs. Davies and Miss Hatch, Your Grace. Mrs. Davies also assisted you when you were injured."

"Then I shall extend my offer to them as well, and they can serve as your chaperones."

"Why would I need chaperones? No one cares about the reputation of a seamstress."

He rose from his chair and walked around the great oak desk, twisting the gold signet ring he wore on his little finger. "I think it's best if you and your dog and neighbors stay here until I can have a word with Grayson. Possibly afterward, too. If you're here, you're out of his reach. Safe. And chaperones protect my reputation as well as yours."

"Stay...here? Loup, too?"

"You named your dog Loo?"

"No...I..." She stopped, then lifted her eyes to his face. "His name is Artie, but sometimes I call him Loup Garou."

"You call your dog Werewolf?" How was it a seamstress came to know an old French legend?

"At times his expressions are almost human," she replied, smiling for the first time since they'd met. "Might I be dismissed, Your Grace? I'll need to gather my things, as will Mrs. Davies and Miss Hatch."

Rhuddlan leaned back against his desk, studying her face. "Of course. I'll send a couple of footmen with you for protection and a carriage will come for the three of you and your things in a few hours. Will that be sufficient time to prepare?"

She nodded quickly. "For me, yes, though I can't speak for my neighbors."

"Of course." He strode across the room and pulled a cord, summoning a servant to the door of the office.

Orders were given to prepare chambers and ready carriages, and Miss Stone was escorted out.

Vaughn came in a few minutes later carrying a stack of papers, a frown on both his mouth and his brow.

"Out with it," Rhuddlan said, leaning back in his chair.

Vaughn didn't dissemble. "Miss Stone is to be your guest, Your Grace?"

"Yes."

"Are you sure that's wise?"

Rhuddlan slid his fingers into his hair and touched the healing wound. Vaughn had asked the same question before Rhuddlan had ridden out the day he was attacked. "Clearly I do, or I wouldn't have extended the invitation. But you have misgivings, I see."

"Not about the lady herself, Your Grace," Vaughn replied quickly. "But if she's the object of Sir George Grayson's affection—"

Rhuddlan held up a hand, cutting off his secretary before the man could finish his thought. "First of all, if threatening the life of a woman is how Grayson expresses affection there is something grossly wrong with him. Secondly, Miss Stone is my tenant and therefore my responsibility. And thirdly, were you listening at the door?"

Vaughn swallowed hard. "Oh no, Your Grace. Sir George is briefly mentioned in the investigator's report on Miss Stone, and I know him by reputation."

"You think he's trouble?"

"I think you have enough trouble of your own to deal with," Vaughn said slowly. "You don't need to invite more."

Rhuddlan rose from his chair and came around the large desk, pacing around the open space in the room. "And you think sheltering Miss Stone will encourage Grayson to come knocking on my door."

"Yes, Your Grace." Vaughn was pale, his posture rigid. "Did he really threaten to kill Miss Stone?"

"That is what she alleges," Rhuddlan replied, pausing at the window to flick back the heavy curtain for a glance outside. "And I believe her. I've promised to speak with Grayson on her behalf."

Vaughn, still in his place near the door, sucked in a quiet breath and Rhuddlan turned away from the window. "You think that's a mistake?"

"No, Your Grace," Vaughn replied, his voice firm. "As you said, Miss Stone is your responsibility. But perhaps, after you've seen to Sir George, you might consider disappearing for a while."

"Nonsense," he scoffed, stalking back over to his desk. "There is far too much to do for me to run off and hide."

Vaughn lifted his chin, meeting Rhuddlan's gaze head on. "Don't forget, Your Grace, that your lawful heir is Lord Nicholas."

And Nick would use the dukedom as his own personal bank—to hell with the welfare of its people. "For now," Rhuddlan returned. Unless he sired a son, there was no way to stop his brother from inheriting the title. But not all of the dukedom's assets were entailed. "And while that is the case, perhaps we should have another look at my will."

"Yes, Your Grace," Vaughn replied. "Would you like me to fetch your copy from the strongbox? Or do you want to go through your correspondence first?"

"Leave the correspondence—I'll start going through it while you go to the strongbox."

"As you wish." Vaughn placed his stack of papers on Rhuddlan's desk and let himself out.

Rhuddlan dumped himself back into his chair and started to reach for his wound again, but thought better of it. It would likely heal faster if he left it be, though that philosophy hadn't worked so well with is brother. Or George Grayson, for that matter.

"I hope I have enough strength to deal with them both," he murmured, straightening up and sorting through the pile of correspondence. "My life is not the only one that depends on it."

"No." Mrs. Davies crossed her arms over her chest and set her mouth in a hard frown.

Olivia looked to Miss Hatch, standing beside her companion in their small parlor.

"Stay in the same house as the Duke of Rhuddlan?" She shook her head. "Not me."

Olivia threw up her hands and turned away. "I understand how you feel about His Grace, but you must realize the danger we're in." She turned back, pointing alternately to the two footmen in blood red livery trimmed in black standing guard, one in front of the little cottage and one in the back. "They aren't here for decoration."

Mrs. D. came forward, holding out her hands and clasping Olivia's. "Oh, dear, we know that. We've both seen firsthand what Sir George has done to you."

"Then why are you fighting this?" Olivia asked, the exasperation evident in her voice. She took a deep breath and tried again, clinging to Mrs. D.'s hands. "I know you're wary of His Grace, but we'll only be there for a few days at the most, and we'll likely only deal with servants. You'll never have to see the duke, and I won't have to worry about what Sir George might do to you." She paused again, swallowing hard. "Who will look after Artie if something happens to you?"

Miss Hatch made a little choking sound and Mrs. D. turned without letting go of Olivia. They exchanged a look, and Mrs. D. had tears in her eyes when she turned back. "You really believe George Grayson will kill you, don't you?"

"Yes," Olivia replied, trying to ignore the catch in her voice. "I'm afraid of what he'll do to the both of you, too."

"And you think we'll be safe at Rhuddlan Hall."

"Yes," Olivia repeated more firmly. "I don't know what His Grace is going to do, but I know Sir George can't get to us there."

Mrs. D. glanced back at Miss H. one more time, then nodded to Olivia. "All right, then. We'll gather our things."

"Thank you." Olivia hugged Mrs. D. tightly, then hugged Miss Hatch, too.

Olivia walked next door with one of the footmen and gathered her own things, taking care to bring Artie's few possessions along as well. The carriage arrived as promised, and the three ladies arranged themselves inside while the footmen stowed their luggage. Artie hopped in last, climbing up on the seat beside his mistress and whacking her with his wagging tail as he looked out the window.

"Do you think he knows what's happening?" Miss Hatch asked with a little smile on her lips.

"He came part of the way home from Belgium in a carriage with Mr. Davies," Olivia told her, trying to stroke Artie's fur and defend against his tail simultaneously. "If he remembers that, he'll know we're to travel somewhere."

The carriage gave a little jolt and rolled forward. "What will he make of Rhuddlan Hall, I wonder?" Mrs. D. said, flattening her hand against the seat to steady herself.

"What will we make of it?" Olivia said, laughing as Artie's ears stood at attention and his nose pressed against the glass. "Have either of you ever been inside?"

Mrs. D. and Miss H both shook their heads, and the conversation shifted to speculation about what exactly they'd find during their short stay at the duke's home. Only a few minutes later they were pulling into the circular drive and coming to a halt. One of the footmen that had been assigned to them opened the carriage door and, after Artie barreled his way out, assisted the three women down.

Olivia whistled to her dog and he came running back, trotting at her side as she was escorted inside the large front door. The first time she'd been here, she'd been half out of her mind with fear and nervousness, and had only seen the corridor and His Grace's study. This time she and her companions were whisked away up a wide staircase to the second floor by a housekeeper who pointed out important items in the house to help the newcomers find their way around. They stopped in what the housekeeper called the guest wing.

"His Grace has said you are to be allowed to choose your bedchambers," she said, gesturing to three open doors. "The two on this side of the corridor connect through a shared sitting room. The doors leading to the sitting room are equipped with locks, should you need them. The one on this side has a slightly larger sitting room, and does not connect to any other suite."

Olivia exchanged looks with Mrs. D. and Miss H. "Would you two like the connecting rooms?"

"If you don't mind, dear," Mrs. D. replied.

"Not at all." In fact, having a chamber all to herself with only one outer door to monitor might give her some of the piece of mind she'd been lacking these past months.

"Very good," the housekeeper said briskly. "I'll have the footmen bring up your things." She turned to walk away, but paused. "Will the, erm, dog be needing anything during your stay?"

Olivia smothered a smile. "He's very well behaved, I assure you. The only thing he'll need is a footman to escort us on our walks. His Grace says I am not to leave the house alone."

The housekeeper shot a skeptical glance at Artie, who had wandered into the suite his mistress had chosen as her own and was giving the sitting room a vigorous inspection. "I'll see to it."

"Thank you," Olivia said, letting her smile break through.

The housekeeper nodded and headed back toward the staircase, leaving the three guests to explore their new, if temporary, home.

Olivia's sitting room was decorated in shades of gold, which ought to have been ostentatious but somehow wasn't. There was a small fire crackling in the fireplace, banishing the autumn chill from the room, and two beautifully carved chairs set before it. Near the large windows sat a small, upholstered settee positioned to take advantage of the sunlight pouring in.

"That is where I shall work," she said, gesturing to Artie as he came to meet her at the door. "Do you think you can keep off the furniture here?"

He wagged his tail in response, lifting his head for a scratch which Olivia obligingly gave him.

Never in her life had Olivia been in a house so grand, let alone invited to stay. But watching bits of fur loosen wherever her fingers traveled filled her with horror—they were going to get dog hair all over His Grace's beautiful carpets!

"Maybe we can ask for a blanket for you," she said, brushing her hands together to slough off the fur sticking to them. He gave himself a little shake and went to one of the windows, pressing his nose against the sparkling clean glass, and Olivia sighed. "Are you so untidy at home? Or do I simply not notice anymore?"

A footman arrived then with her luggage, and she set about making the suite feel more like home. She hadn't had much to bring so the effort didn't take much time, and soon Olivia had settled herself on the settee with the dress she was finishing for one of her long-time customers.

After two days of sewing, sometimes with Mrs. D. and Miss H. sitting by the fire, sometimes with just Artie snoring softly in the sun, Olivia began to ask the footmen who took turns escorting her outdoors with Artie if they knew anything about her situation. They deflected her questions, as she'd expected.

"Do you think he's forgotten about us?" Mrs. D. asked as they took their after dinner tea in Olivia's sitting room.

Miss H. snorted. "This place is certainly large enough. He could house a school for the entire village here and never even notice the students."

"That's not all that far from the truth," Olivia laughed. "But I'm sure His Grace hasn't forgotten about us. He's a busy man."

The two older women exchanged a look, but neither said anything else.

That night, Olivia sat at the beautiful maple writing desk situated inside her bedchamber and wrote two short notes: one to Mr. Vaughn to inquire whether or not she could schedule an appointment with the duke, and one to His Grace to ask if he'd made any progress with Sir George.

She gave both notes to the footman who arrived for Artie's morning walk, and he promised to deliver them to their respective recipients. But the rest of the morning, then the entire afternoon passed with no word from either man.

Finally, after three days of waiting, Olivia was ushered into the duke's dim study. "Have you any news, Your Grace? Not that we aren't grateful for your generous hospitality, but my neighbors and I are looking forward to returning to our own homes."

"I suspect Artie will be happy to return, as well," the duke returned with a small smile. "The footmen tell me he's been patrolling your wing of the house like a sentry. You ought to call him Cerberus instead of Loup Garou."

Olivia stifled a grin. Artie had also been pestering every servant that came his way, sniffing and following and demanding attention. "All your servants have been very kind to him, which I appreciate very much."

"It's good to have a dog about the place again," His Grace said amiably. He opened his mouth to continue, but was cut off when the door flew open.

"Your Grace!"

"Mr. Lewis, what is the meaning of this? I am not to be disturbed!"

"It's Mr. Vaughn," the interloper continued. "He's been attacked."

Chapter Three

Once Rhuddlan sent Miss Stone back to her chamber and calmed Lewis, one of his regiment of secretaries, the details began to emerge. Vaughn had apparently been meeting with one of Rhuddlan's investigators off the estate and had been set upon during his journey back. A tenant farmer had found him by the side of the road, beaten within an inch of his life but with just enough strength left to ask for his employer.

"How many attackers?" Rhuddlan asked quietly, behind the closed door of his study.

"Mr. Vaughn wasn't sure," Lewis answered. "But it was more than one. He's in a bad way, Your Grace."

Rhuddlan felt a scowl forming on his features. Who would attack a man in broad daylight? "Send Bates for the physician, and tell him to take Hermes."

Lewis nodded and made for the study door. Hermes was the fastest horse in the Rhuddlan stables and Bates, the head groom, was one of the few men who could control him at full speed.

"Lewis?"

The man froze with his hand on the doorknob. "Yes, Your Grace?"

"Where is Vaughn now?"

"Sanders offered up his own chamber."

Rhuddlan gave a short nod of approval. The butler's quarters were easier to carry a bleeding man to than any of the guest chambers. "Good. I'll go to him myself in a moment."

Lewis hurried out the door and Rhuddlan took a moment to collect himself. Was this simply more bad luck? Or the work of his brother? Was Vaughn's connection with Rhuddlan the reason he was targeted? He swore under his breath. Maybe Vaughn's suggestion to disappear wasn't as ridiculous as he'd at first thought.

Rhuddlan found his principle secretary lying in Sanders's bed, quiet and still with bruises already forming on the exposed skin that wasn't bloody, his eyes closed. For the briefest of moments Rhuddlan thought the man had already died, and a wave of guilt crashed over him. But then Vaughn took a shallow breath and Rhuddlan took his own, deeper one.

"Mr. Vaughn," he said, keeping his voice low even though the room was devoid of other people. Vaughn struggled on the bed as if he were trying to sit up, but Rhuddlan laid a hand on his shoulder. "No need for that. You just be still and rest—the physician is on his way."

"I'm sorry, Your Grace," Vaughn croaked slowly. "I thought I was careful..."

"This is not your fault," Rhuddlan said firmly.

Vaughn moved restlessly on the bed. "I should have been more discreet..."

"This is not your fault," Rhuddlan repeated. "I will have questions for you about who did this—" Vaughn opened his mouth to speak, but Rhuddlan patted his shoulder "—later. The only thing I want you to do right now is focus on healing. You follow whatever instructions the physician gives you, and don't worry about anything else."

Vaughn licked his bleeding lips. "Yes, Your Grace," he said with what sounded like reluctance.

Rhuddlan pressed his lips together. How could he ease his secretary's mind? "I need you hale and hearty again, Mr. Vaughn. Without you to keep me organized, I'm not sure how I'll manage the dukedom."

The secretary offered a painful smile. "That's kind of you to say, Your Grace."

"Kind, but also true." Rhuddlan stood awkwardly beside the bed for what was surely one of the longest moments of his life. What else could he say to this man to distract him a bit from the pain? "You know the clerks in my employ better than anyone—who do you recommend I lean on while you recuperate?"

"Mr. Lewis," Vaughn answered with a half suppressed grimace, shifting his body gingerly into a more comfortable position. "He will see you through until I can return to my post."

Rhuddlan heard the door swing open behind him, and turned to find his personal physician entering the room. "Thank you," he said, turning back to his secretary. "Now you remember what I said about following the doctor's orders. Lewis and I will muddle through until you are well."

After a brief word with the physician Rhuddlan went back to his study, towing Lewis along behind him. After informing the man of his temporary promotion and conveying his duties for the rest of the day, Rhuddlan sent him off to begin his work. He waited a few minutes more for the physician to report back—a couple of broken bones and at least one blow to the head, but the lacerations were mostly superficial—then took himself off to the village with clenched fists. Anger and frustration were boiling inside him, and he needed an outlet—something that he could fix quickly and easily to regain his sense of control.

It wasn't difficult to find Sir George Grayson. Rhuddlan stopped at the village tavern, ordered a tankard of ale, and carried it to the table in the corner indicated by the publican's daughter.

"Mind if I join you?"

Grayson's head came up slowly, then jerked the rest of the way when he saw who was standing before him. "Certainly, Your Grace."

"Then you know who I am."

"I do. To what do I owe this honor?" Grayson smiled at him, a sort of half smile that looked as though its wearer was trying to be modest.

"I'm not sure how much of an honor you'll think it after I've said what I came to say," Rhuddlan replied, taking a drink of his ale as he seated himself opposite his quarry.

The smile didn't waver. "And what is that?"

Rhuddlan had decided on the way over to simply be direct. "I want to talk about Olivia Stone."

The smile grew and Grayson leaned back in his chair. "My betrothed."

"Not according to her."

The smoke from the fireplace drifted toward them, tainting the air with a slightly sooty quality, but Grayson appeared not to notice. "She just needs a little encouragement."

"It was encouragement, then, when you threatened to kill her and her dog?" Rhuddlan asked through clenched teeth.

Grayson laughed and lifted his own tankard. "Is that what she told you?" he replied after taking a drink. "I always knew she was prone to exaggeration, but I never thought she would stray that far from reality."

"A hysterical female then?" Rhuddlan said, squeezing the handle of his tankard.

"Yes she is, Your Grace, and I apologize for her. It sounds as if she's wasted your time with tales of my villainy, when I've only been trying to help her."

Rhuddlan grunted. What he really wanted to do was smash his fist into the knight's face, but as satisfying as that would be, it wouldn't accomplish anything. Yet. "She doesn't need your help," he said in a growly voice.

"Are you— Are you warning me off?" Grayson asked, leaning forward over the table. "Do you think to steal my woman from me, Your Grace?"

"Even if she were a possession and not a person, I cannot steal from you what isn't yours," Rhuddlan countered, bending forward. "Miss Stone has made it clear that she does not wish to ever see you again."

Grayson leaned further forward, his nose almost touching Rhuddlan's. "Is that so?"

"It is," Rhuddlan said in what his brother used to call his Deadly Calm Duke Voice. "And here's something to keep in mind, *Sir* George. I command the largest network of informants in the realm, which means that no matter where you are, there is likely someone in my pay close by." He reached over and grabbed the man by his cravat and gave it a little twist. "If you so much as breathe the same air as Miss Stone, I will know about it."

"And what are you going to do if I keep courting her?" Grayson asked, grinning. "Have some ruffians beat me?"

An image of Vaughn's bloodied body flashed across Rhuddlan's mind and a wave of anger washed over him. He again pushed the fire down and called upon his cold, calculating side. "No, that's much too easy. I'll come for you myself. And no one will ever know what happened to you," he said with a tiny smile on his lips.

Grayson swallowed hard, his Adam's apple bobbing in his throat, but tried to maintain his veneer of bravado. "What are you going to do, kill me? That's a capital offense."

"But who would prosecute me?" Rhuddlan asked with genuine curiosity. "Have your friends or family the power and money to oppose me?" Even in the dim light, Rhuddlan could see the color draining from his adversary's face and he let his smile grow slightly, relaxing his hold on Grayson's cravat. "Besides, there can't be a prosecution if no one ever finds your body."

"What?" The word was more of a croak than proper English.

"Did you ever meet my cousin Rhys?" Rhuddlan asked, settling back into his chair as if to tell a story. For once his black reputation might work in his favor. "He, too, decided he could flout my authority."

Grayson's eyes widened slightly. The whole of Society knew about the argument between Rhuddlan and Rhys Blake that occurred just days before the latter seemingly vanished from the face of the earth. They knew that Rhys owned a piece of property Rhuddlan had long coveted, and that Rhys's son sold it to Rhuddlan shortly after his father's disappearance. The rumor mill had filled in the blanks with its own speculation which, judging by the blatant fear creeping into his expression, George Grayson was very familiar with.

Grayson shrugged his shoulders, trying and failing to brush off Rhuddlan's implications. "I don't know why you're getting so wound up over an insignificant little tart like Olivia, but if you want my leavings, who am I to say no?"

My leavings. Rhuddlan nearly unleashed his fist then, but held himself in check. Grayson was promising, in his own ugly way, to leave Miss Stone in peace. Rhuddlan's words had done their job—the knight was clearly terrified. Throwing a punch would only make Rhuddlan seem human again, and would likely result in Grayson terrorizing Miss Stone even more.

But if he came within five miles of her...

"Excellent," he said instead, lifting his tankard to his lips for a long drink. "I'll hold you to that."

Rhuddlan rose from the table and strode to the door, forcing his body to move at an easy pace. He made his way to the stables, stripping off his tailcoat and cravat while the ostler brought his stallion, Hermes, around. He held the horse back until they'd reached the edge of the village, then he let the animal have its head.

Perhaps, if his horse ran fast enough and long enough, Rhuddlan's pent up emotions would blow away in the wind.

Olivia sat in the sitting room connected to the bedchamber she temporarily called her own, her needle flashing in the sunlight that shone brightly through the windows as she mended shirts for old Mr. Jones. A widower who'd elected not to marry a second time, he'd been her steadiest customer since she'd arrived in Wales, paying her for her services partly in coin and partly in fresh eggs laid by the three hens he kept. Mrs. D. and Miss H. sat together in front of the empty fireplace, exchanging smiles as Mrs. D. read aloud the latest letter from her daughter in Kent.

A knock on the door sounded, and Artie, who had been snoring contentedly in a shaft of sunlight, bounded to his feet and began to bark.

Mrs. D. glanced over at Olivia. "Were you expecting someone this afternoon?"

"No one knows I'm here," she answered, shaking her head and rising from her chair. She set Mr. Jones's shirt aside and, with a shrug of her shoulders, went to answer the door. "Loup, go to Mrs. D." Olivia waited until her dog complied, quiet but only half-sitting, ready to spring into action should he be needed.

Olivia swung the door open, expecting a maid or footman, perhaps with news about poor Mr. Vaughn.

"Miss Stone, may I speak to you for a moment?"

Olivia's mouth dropped open. There before her stood the Duke of Rhuddlan with nary a servant in sight. "Erm, yes, of course, Your Grace," she stuttered, opening the door wider to gesture him inside.

"I know this is unusual," he continued, nodding briefly at Mrs. D. and Miss H. when they popped up from their seats and dropped curtsies, "but the subject we must discuss is rather delicate, and I thought it best to do so somewhere other than my study."

"Will you sit?" Olivia asked, falling back on behavior that had been drilled into her from infancy and resuming her seat. No matter their rank, a gentleman would never sit before a lady did.

The duke swished his coattails back and settled on a large ottoman, his hands coming to rest on his knees. Mrs. D. and Miss H. each began to stand, but His Grace held up a hand to stay the motion. "Sit, please. This may also concern you both."

Mrs. D.'s eyes widened and she once again shot a what's-happening look at Olivia, but she resumed her seat. Not in time to catch Artie, however, who had decided this newcomer needed to be investigated.

"I have a proposal for your consideration, Miss Stone," the duke began, holding his hand out for Artie to sniff.

Olivia sat up a little straighter, willing her dog to behave himself. "And what is that, Your Grace?"

"That we disappear together for a time," he answered.

Olivia looked for any hint of a smile, the tiniest pull at the corners of his mouth, but found nothing. "Disappear?"

He nodded once, running a hand down Artie's back as the dog continued his inspection. "I will quietly escort you to your cousin in Liverpool. If he's a good man he'll see to your comfort and safety, and you'll never have to worry about George Grayson again."

"Did it go so badly with Sir George?" she asked, trying valiantly to keep her voice from shaking. If the most powerful man in Wales was urging her to flee, things could not have gone well.

"He is unpredictable," the duke said with a frown. Artie's nose was pressed against His Grace's trouser leg by this point, the dog having latched onto some enticing smell, but the man seemed not to notice. "I believe I've shown him the hell that awaits him should he ever come near you again. But he may also risk my wrath and seek retribution against you for my intervention."

Olivia pushed away her manners and leaned back in her chair, blowing out a breath. "I was afraid of that. But my cousin's home is the first place he'll look when he figures out that I've gone away."

"He knows of your cousin?"

It was Olivia's turn to nod. "My family connection is the only reason Sir George wants to wed me—I am somewhat distantly related to Lord Teverton, and Sir George wants very badly to be an aristocrat."

"Ah, I see." His Grace's hand seemed to clamp a little tighter on his knee, but his free hand remained on Artie's back. "I don't know Teverton personally, but I know of him. If he's any kind of gentleman, he'll do right by you. If he turns you away," the duke continued before Olivia could ask the question that had plagued her for months, "then I will see to your comfort and safety. All three of you."

"Because we helped you?" Mrs. D. asked in a small voice.

"In part," the duke acknowledged. "But also because you are my tenants, my responsibility. And because in allowing me to take you to Liverpool, you would be doing me a favor."

Olivia tilted her head slightly to one side. "How would *we* be doing *you* a favor? It's not as if you'd be tagging along on a trip we were already planning to make, Your Grace. To be frank, I doubt I possess the funds to even get to Teverton on my own, let alone purchase food and lodging along the way."

The Duke of Rhuddlan studied her for a long moment, his green eyes trained on her face as if he could see every lie she'd ever told written there on her skin. Then he blinked, appearing to have come to some conclusion. "You likely heard about the mill that burned down." He paused, continuing on after she'd nodded. "And you witnessed the attack on me. There have been other...incidents...as well."

"Oh dear," Miss Hatch murmured from her seat by the fireplace.

"Indeed," the duke said, briefly turning in her direction. "The prevailing hypothesis is that if I were to leave the estate for a while, these incidents of violence would follow me."

"So if you leave the estate discreetly and tell no one where you are going, you're hoping these incidents will stop all together," Olivia supplied.

"Exactly," he said, stabbing a finger into the air.

Olivia shifted her gaze from the duke to her neighbors and lifted her eyebrows in question. What did they think of all this? Their association with her put them in Sir George's path, and they'd both benefit from the Duke of Rhuddlan's assurances. But if they thought him evil...

His Grace must have read her look as hesitation, because he added, "I promised to ensure your safety and comfort should Teverton fail to do his familial duty. I will also stand by my promise to see you safe from George Grayson for as long as he is a threat to you."

"Thank you, Your Grace," Olivia said, reflexively offering him an appreciative smile.

"But you would like specifics," he added for her, ruffling the thick fur on the scruff of Artie's neck as the dog finally gave up sniffing and sat down beside the ottoman.

"Yes," she replied, sounding both eager and wary at the same time. Her life had been filled with little more than uncertainty since her parents' deaths, and she wasn't about to pin her hopes for security on empty promises.

He shifted on the ottoman. "You may retain possession of your cottage, rent free, for the remainder of your life."

The sound of Olivia's in-drawn breath sounded like a roar in the silence that followed His Grace's pronouncement. A life interest in her home would effectively make her independent, regardless of her cousin's potential generosity or lack thereof. It would mean she could turn away Sir George's advances without fear of becoming homeless and starving.

"My cottage *and* protection from Sir George?" she asked in a half-whisper.

"That is correct."

"And all I have to do is travel with you to Liverpool?"

"Yes. Your neighbors—" he gestured to Mrs. D. and Miss H, who were perched on the edge of their seats, clasping hands "—might also want to come along. They would likely be targeted by Grayson in your place."

Olivia found herself shaking her head. "Why would you do this for me? For us?"

"Because you shouldn't be forced to marry a man you fear," he answered quietly. "And no one should be harmed because a man's advances have been rebuffed."

"You are kind to say so," she managed around the lump forming in her throat. "Many gentlemen would disagree with you."

"Not in my hearing," he quipped with a half-smile. "And it's not as though there's no risk to you three. Anyone with a connection to the dukedom of Rhuddlan is a potential target for whoever is committing these violent attacks."

Olivia let her gaze slide to her friends once more, before meeting the duke's eyes. "May we have a moment for discussion, Your Grace?"

"Of course," he replied, giving Artie one last pat before rising. "I will await your decision in my study."

The door had barely closed behind him when Mrs. D. and Miss H. fairly burst from their seats by the fireplace. They weren't smiling exactly, but neither were they outright scowling.

"What do you think?" Olivia asked, looking from one to the other.

"Your own cottage and transportation to Lord Teverton are awfully compelling reasons to agree to this scheme," Mrs. D. said, a note of reluctance in her voice.

Miss H. was shaking her head. "It's too dangerous. If anyone discovers who he is before we reach Lord Teverton..."

"And if we remain in our homes, you might as well get used to calling me Lady Grayson," Olivia returned, trying to keep her tone gentle and not quite succeeding. "For Sir George will see that I submit to him, one way or another."

Miss Hatch squinted at Olivia. "You want to go, don't you?"

"Yes," Olivia said resolutely. "If Lord Teverton does indeed agree to help me, then I will no longer have to live my life in fear of displeasing Sir George, and neither will you. If he declines my request for assistance, I will still have my cottage and we will be under the Duke of Rhuddlan's protection."

"When you put it that way," Mrs. D. said, her frown deepening, "it sounds like an easy decision. But the duke himself said it was dangerous to be linked to him. What if something happens to you?"

"If I don't take this chance, George Grayson will kill one of us. I have no doubt about that." Olivia swallowed hard. She'd been reluctant to say the words aloud, but the thought had been there in the back of her mind for weeks. "I couldn't live with myself if something happened to either of you that I could have prevented."

"You stop blaming yourself this instant," Mrs. D. said firmly. "Sir George is responsible for his actions and no one else."

Miss H. laid a hand on her companion's shoulder. "You're both right," she said, her eyes moving from Mrs. D. to Olivia. "If Sir George burns down our home, it would not be your fault. But if there is something we can do to try to keep ourselves safe from him, then we should do it."

Mrs. D. looked sideways at Miss. H. "You want to travel with Lord Ruthven?"

Olivia suppressed a laugh. Lord Ruthven was the main character—a nobleman-turned-vampire—in the book they'd read aloud together not so long ago. "Is that how you think of His Grace?" she asked instead. "As a conniving, deceitful demon? Even though he's taken us in to his own home to protect us?"

"He is not all that he seems," was the only thing she would say, clamping her mouth shut and crossing her arms over her chest.

"And yet, I think he is our best hope," Miss Hatch replied gently. "Our only other choice is to deal with Sir George ourselves."

A shiver coursed through Olivia despite the warmth from the sun still shining in the windows. Mrs. Davies must have seen it, for she relaxed her mouth and her arms.

"When you put it that way, I cannot argue." She pointed a finger at Olivia. "But you had better get all His Grace's promises in writing, before witnesses."

"A good piece of advice," Olivia replied with a nod. "I will be sure to do that."

"Then we are agreed?" Miss Hatch asked, looking once again from Mrs. D. to Olivia. "We will travel with the Duke of Rhuddlan to Liverpool and meet your cousin."

"And be rid of Sir George's threats once and for all," Olivia added with more conviction than she felt. The duke was her last best hope, certainly. And if he upheld the promises he'd already made to her, she should be able to live out the rest of her life in obscure peace and quiet.

But what if he found out who she really was and what she'd done?

Chapter Four

IT WAS TWO more days before they could depart. Rhuddlan posted letters to both his good friend the Duke of Sussex and Teverton while they made their preparations. The letter to Teverton explained Miss Stone's situation and included a note in her own hand. The letter to Sussex contained a request for assistance —Sussex was the older brother of Nick's patron, the Duke of Cumberland, and wielded a fair amount of power as a son of the king. Rhuddlan hoped Sussex might be able to rein in his brother, allowing Rhuddlan to deal with his own brother unimpeded.

There was also the matter of the guise he and Miss Stone would travel under. They had decided to pose as cousins on their way to visit an ailing grandmother, but Miss Stone's wardrobe was not of the same quality as even Rhuddlan's shabbiest clothing. Fortunately, Rhuddlan Hall's housekeeper was of approximately the same shape and had been persuaded to give up two of her best gowns—castoffs from Rhuddlan's aunt—for Miss Stone to alter as necessary.

A hundred other things had to be done before the women and canine could at last climb into a plain carriage—one where the Rhuddlan arms had been painted over—and Rhuddlan could mount Hermes. Fortunately, their first day of travel passed without incident, and they found a modest but clean inn to stay the night.

They took two rooms, one for Rhuddlan and one for the women, and had supper and wash water brought up. He expected that to be the end of his interaction with anyone other than his own staff, but there was soon a light knock on his chamber door.

He opened it to find Mrs. Davies standing on the other side with Miss Stone. She was wrapped in a dark cloak, a dog lead in one hand and the dog himself standing beside her.

"Good evening, Cousin," Miss Stone said lightly. "May we come in for a moment?"

"Certainly." Rhuddlan stepped aside, allowing the women to enter and Artie to sniff him. He shut the door behind him and turned, raising his eyebrows in an unasked question.

Miss Stone stepped forward, sliding something off her finger. "I believe this is yours."

The object she handed him was a gold signet ring engraved with a stylized dragon, a gift from his father on the occasion of Rhuddlan's twenty-first birthday. He'd taken it off for this trip, not wanting it to give away his real identity. But he also had not wanted to leave it behind—it was possible that he'd actually need to confirm his identity, either by simply possessing the ring, or by sealing a letter with it.

"The coachman was out when we took Artie for a walk," she went on. "He thought you might like to keep it for the night rather than leave it in your luggage."

"Yes, thank you." He took the ring from her and slid it onto his little finger, a small part of him sighing in relief. He'd felt rather strange without it all day. Artie, as he had each time they'd stopped to change horses, was already sniffing him and Rhuddlan reached down to give him a pat. "Did you enjoy your walk?"

Miss Stone grinned then attempted, not quite successfully, to smother it. "He is cross with me for not letting him chase the squirrels."

As she spoke, the dog pulled himself free and trotted over to the fireplace, dragging his lead behind him. "Artie, no..."

"He's all right there," Rhuddlan said with a smile as the dog laid down before the fire. "He needs to gather himself after being denied a chance at those squirrels. Perhaps you both would like a cup of tea while he rests?"

Miss Stone glanced at Mrs. Davies, who pressed her lips together but gave a small nod. "Thank you, Your Grace. We would like that."

She poured cups for each of them, waiting for Mrs. Davies to settle in the room's only chair before seating herself on the bed. Rhuddlan elected to stand. Sitting on the bed beside Miss Stone, even though it was the only seat left, felt too intimate.

The conversation was pleasant, though. She described Artie's attempt to break free and chase two squirrels through the bustling courtyard, thwarted by his lead and the quick-thinking coachman. He talked of Vaughn's recovery, slow though it was going to be, and the care his wife, who had been invited to stay with her husband at Rhuddlan Hall, lovingly provided.

"You've got quite the tender heart, Your Grace," Miss Stone said with a soft smile.

"It's Mr. Blake for the duration of this trip," he reminded her quietly. The inn was well kept and highly regarded, but the walls were thin. "Or Cousin Lucas if you think it appropriate."

"Yes, of course," she replied in a half-whisper. "I'd forgotten for a moment."

He had as well, though he was loath to say it aloud. "No matter. We must both simply resolve to be more careful."

"Which we will do. But don't think I'll forget that you're housing an employee and his wife in your home as if they were honored guests," she replied, her smile returning.

"Vaughn's condition does not allow him to be moved," Rhuddlan said, setting his teacup on the tray it had arrived on. "The easiest way for them to continue to be together was to bring her to him."

Her eyes—blue like the butterflies they'd seen flitting through the meadows earlier in the day—held his for a long moment. "There's your tender heart again, Mr. Blake."

"No one will ever believe you if you tell them."

Miss Stone gestured with her chin to Mrs. Davies, who was slumped in her chair with her chin resting on her chest. "She certainly won't, but I rather like knowing something no one else does."

"She tries to protect you as if you were her daughter," he observed, settling himself at the foot of the bed. The day spent in the saddle was starting to take its toll and he was tiring. "Miss Hatch, too, but not to the same extent."

Miss Stone nodded. "Mrs. D. has a daughter about my age who is married to a farmer in Kent. I think doting on me helps ease her worry when the distance starts to feel overwhelming."

"And you aren't all on your own."

Miss Stone's mouth curved into a soft smile. "It's a good arrangement for both of us. What about you, Your Grace? Who takes care of you?"

"Vaughn is practically my nursemaid some days," he replied, surprised to be answering her smile with one of his own. Then it faded as a memory bubbled up to the surface. "My wife looked after me fairly well when she was alive, though it's been..." He paused, mentally counting the passage of time. "...ten years now since she died."

"I'm so sorry." The words were soft, the hand she held out to him even softer when he clasped it. "Were you married long?"

There were no witnesses, and with Miss Stone's other neighbor snoring in the room next door, no one to rush in and catch him "compromising" her. Rhuddlan allowed himself to slide closer to her, to accept her sympathy as genuine, resting their joined hands on his thigh as if they belonged there together. "A few years. It was a political marriage, but we were fond of each other."

She gave his hand a slight squeeze. "I won't ask if you've thought of re-marrying. Even if you haven't, at least half of the *ton* has."

Ah, then she knew something of Society. But he couldn't figure out who her parents might have been. "Have you participated in the Marriage Mart?"

"Once or twice," she said, shifting her eyes away from his. "I didn't take."

"I find that hard to believe." Her figure was curvier, more rounded than the current willowy fashion and her dowry probably hadn't been large. But she was intelligent and well mannered, not to mention an attractive armful of a woman. Surely someone would have proposed marriage to her.

"Well, it's true. I am still Miss Stone after all."

Her words were clipped, her tone flat. Rhuddlan wanted to know what had happened during her time but decided not to press the subject. Instead, he asked about something he knew she'd enjoy discussing.

"How long have you and Artie been together?"

As he'd hoped, her face brightened instantly and she glanced over at the dog stretched out before the fire. "Mrs. D.'s husband brought him home from Belgium. He found this young pup running around on the battlefield after Waterloo, thin and mangy, and toted him back to camp. Mr. Davies fed him and cleaned him up, and his captain's wife looked after the dog when Mr. D. couldn't."

"Then 'Artie' came from Wellington?" Rhuddlan asked with a short laugh. How would old Nosey react if he knew a dog had been named for him?

Miss Stone grinned. "Mr. D. thought he should give the dog a strong name so he'd grow to be a strong dog. It worked—Artie filled out and Mr. D. discovered he wasn't a puppy after all, just underfed."

"How did he end up with you?"

"He kept trying to herd the Maxwells' sheep," she said, her features soft when she glanced at Artie again.

"They live a couple of miles away and have just a small flock, but every morning Artie would run over there like his life depended on it. Mr. and Mrs. Maxwell were not terribly pleased to have a strange dog hanging around their livelihood from sunup to sundown, but Artie clearly needed something to keep him busy. Mr. Davies thought that perhaps Artie would take to guarding me instead of the sheep, and Mrs. Davies thought I'd be safer with a big dog around."

Rhuddlan stroked his thumb over the back of her hand. "It seems they were both right."

"To an extent," she said, swinging her gaze back to him. In the light of the fire her lips were full and tempting. "He herds me more than he guards me," she continued with a little laugh, "but I probably am safer when he's with me. Who would contend with an animal nearly seven stone who looks more wolf than hound, just to get to me?"

"Only those whom Master Artie approves of, would be my guess," he said, giving her hand a little squeeze. Perhaps it was the firelight and the affection she held for her dog, or it could have been the danger of their situation stimulating his senses, but the idea of kissing Miss Stone drifted into his mind. And this time it sounded like an excellent idea.

Her full lips pulled into another smile and she squeezed his hand in return. "You've guessed correctly. You seem to have met his high standards, too."

"Have I met yours?" he asked quietly, leaning toward her a little.

"You have so far," she murmured.

Rhuddlan closed the distance between them and brushed his lips over hers. She squeezed his hand again, and he took that as a sign that she wanted to continue. Sliding a little closer, he cupped her face gently in his free hand and captured her bottom lip between his.

An instant later, he realized something was wrong. She was still, rigid, not the warm, welcoming female he'd expected.

"I do apologize, Miss Stone," he said, drawing away. "I thought perhaps you wanted me to kiss you, but it seems I was mistaken."

Her shadowed eyes met his for the briefest of moments before she dropped her gaze to the mattress they sat on. "It is I who should apologize, Your Grace," she said, her voice slightly strained. "I did want you to kiss me, but then..."

"You don't owe me an explanation," he replied with a shake of his head. "Not wanting to be kissed is reason enough to stop."

"You— you're not angry?"

"Angry because you don't want to kiss me? Of course not." He released her hand and offered her a smile. "I'm a little disappointed, but that's my problem."

"You don't think me a tease?" she asked in a small voice. Her breathing was rapid and he noticed her other hand was gripping the coverlet, but he didn't think it was suppressed passion coursing through her body. It looked like fear.

And he was going to make George Grayson pay for it.

Rhuddlan moved away, back toward the foot of the bed, just in time to see Mrs. Davies's eyes blinking open.

"Ah, there she is," Miss Stone said lightly, her gaze shifting from Rhuddlan to her neighbor. "Perhaps we'd better retire for the evening."

"As should I," he replied, rising and offering his hand to help her up off the bed. "I'll bid you good night, then."

Her eyes met his and held them for just a moment, then she smiled. "Good night to you, too, Mr. Blake."

Olivia was startled from a light sleep by someone banging on her door. Except that, before she could get to her feet, someone who sounded like her faux cousin had answered it. She rubbed her eyes and forced them open, tiptoeing to the door and listening through the thin slab of wood. Someone was in the hallway speaking to His Grace in an agitated manner. She couldn't make out all the words, but it was clear that something was wrong.

"Mrs. D., Miss H., wake up! We must dress!" Olivia whispered hoarsely, shaking her neighbors awake. "Something is wrong and we must be ready."

The women reluctantly awoke, tumbling groggily out of bed and reaching for their gowns. As Olivia pulled on her own clothing, she was grateful for once not to be a lady anymore—she could dress so much faster with clothing that was designed to be put on without help.

By the time a knock—a real one this time—sounded on their door, all three women were in an appropriate state of dress, if not enthusiastic about it.

Olivia crack open the door gave a small sigh of relief when she saw the duke and brushed Artie back from his inquisition. "Come in, Cousin."

He lifted one questioning eyebrow but entered when she opened the door wider. "You heard?"

"I heard someone knocking on your door," Olivia replied, "but not why. What's happened?"

"I believe my brother has found us," he said grimly. "We must leave this place as soon as possible."

Mrs. D.'s eyes were round and Miss H. looked pale in the light of the candle she was holding. But this was not the first time Olivia had awoken in the night prepared to run.

"If we are permitted to take our possessions, we can be ready to depart in just a few minutes," she said, attempting to ignore the pounding of her heart. "If we must leave them, we are ready now."

The duke's gaze swept over the dim room. "We have a few moments before the carriage will be ready. Anything you do not have packed when I call for you will be left behind."

When the door clicked shut behind him, the three women went to work. None of them had brought much, but there were a few things they'd unpacked upon arrival at the inn. Artie, rushing from person to person to see what all the excitement was, ended up getting in the way more often than not and Olivia finally settled him on the bed with a hardened crust of bread left over from the previous night's supper.

But they were ready and waiting when His Grace knocked again on their door. He and the coachman helped the women with their luggage and led them single-file, the duke in front and the coachman at the rear, down the stairs and through the kitchens.

When they reached the rear door of the inn, the Duke of Rhuddlan paused. Go with John Coachman now," he directed the three women. "He'll get you settled, and I'll be along in a minute."

"This way, ladies," the coachman said with a too-cheerful smile.

Mrs. D. and Miss H. followed obediently with Artie, but Olivia hesitated. "What do you mean to do?" she asked the duke.

"The innkeeper has put himself at great risk to warn us. I mean to show my appreciation for that."

He reached into an inner pocket of his tailcoat and pulled out a blank piece of paper with one hand, while the other took the pen the innkeeper was handing him. Bending over a table that had been pushed against one wall, he scratched something out on the paper, pausing only to dip the pen in the inkwell that had been set down beside him. When he was finished, he took up the candle the innkeeper was holding and dripped some wax onto the paper, pressing his signet ring into it.

"When it's safe to do so, take this to Rhuddlan Hall," the duke said, handing the paper to the innkeeper. "Ask for Mr. Vaughn or Mr. Lewis."

The innkeeper glanced down at the paper and his eyes went wide, no doubt noting the signature on the paper. The duke had taken their rooms under the name Lucas Blake, but had signed the note with his full title. "Y-yes, Your Grace."

"Shhhh," the duke said, putting a finger to his lips.

"Oh, yes, of course, *Mr. Blake.*"

His Grace patted the innkeeper on the shoulder. "Good man. We'll cause you no further trouble, now."

Olivia hoped that was true. If Lord Nicholas was anything like Sir George, she hated to think what might happen to the poor innkeeper and his family if Lord Nicholas found out the Duke of Rhuddlan had been here.

His Grace gave the innkeeper a nod and gestured to Olivia to get going. She turned and headed toward the kitchen door, noting with interest that the duke's hand came to rest on the small of her back as he guided her out to their waiting coach.

There wasn't time to think much about it, though— the coachman was coming out to hustle them into their conveyance. It was not the same one they'd arrived in; this one was smaller, painted bright yellow with the arms of an aristocrat she didn't recognize.

"Up you go," the coachman said lightly, handing her in.

Mrs. D. and Miss H. were already seated on the rear-facing bench, with Artie taking up most of the floor. He perked up and lifted his head as Olivia stepped around him, wagging his tail against everyone's legs.

"Were you afraid I wasn't coming?" she asked him, scratching his ears as she took her seat.

"I think he was," Mrs. D. said, glancing at the duke out of the corner of her eye.

"Never fear, Master Artie," His Grace said, stepping into the carriage behind Olivia. "I will see her safe when you can't."

Olivia tried to suppress a smile but wasn't entirely successful. "How lucky I am to have two handsome gentlemen looking after me. And Artie no doubt thanks you, Your Grace."

The duke scratched the dog's neck. "It's my pleasure."

Until Sir George got angry enough to come after her again. Olivia pushed the thought away and offered what she hoped was a genuine-looking smile instead as the carriage lurched forward.

The four of them sat in silence for the first few miles, looking out the windows into what was still a dark landscape. But as time wore on and their interrupted night caught up with them, Mrs. D. and Miss H. drifted back to sleep, leaning against each other for support. Artie, too, seemed to take in the quiet and the swaying of the vehicle, and was soon softly snoring on the floor.

But Olivia couldn't sleep. Her heart had settled into a more normal rhythm and her eyelids were heavy, but she could not calm her mind enough to drift off.

"We are safe, Miss Stone," the duke said softly. "If Nick had seen us, or knew of the carriage switch, he'd already have run us off the road."

"You're certain?"

"As I can be."

"And the innkeeper?"

His Grace sighed. "I don't know. If he managed to put off my brother, he and his family should remain unharmed. Nick won't give them a second thought unless he thinks he was lied to."

Gooseflesh rose on Olivia's skin and she wrapped her arms around herself, jostling the duke slightly in their close quarters. "Let's hope he doesn't suspect."

"From your lips to God's ear."

"Why does your brother want to harm you?" Olivia asked. It was probably an impertinent question, but if she and her friends were in Lord Nicholas's path, she deserved to know why.

"He wants control of the dukedom," His Grace answered, slouching down a bit in his seat, solid and warm beside her. "He is my heir until I produce a son. If I die, he obviously takes control of everything I haven't willed to others. And if I am incapacitated, he can petition for the same power."

"Like the Prince Regent."

The duke nodded slowly. "In that same vein, yes."

"Does he think you incapable?" she asked with curiosity. That was why the Prince of Wales had been appointed Regent, but the Duke of Rhuddlan appeared to be of sound mind.

"He thinks me miserly," His Grace said, pressing his lips together for a moment. "And the Duke of Cumberland thinks Nick is easy to manipulate."

Olivia shuddered. "Is it true that His Grace murdered his valet and had an affair with the man's wife?" It had been several years now, but versions of that story had been printed in newspapers all over the country, including those her father used to read.

Rhuddlan's tight expression loosened at that. "It wouldn't be out of character for him, certainly. And he was so secret about his affairs, he could have been carrying on with Mrs. Sellis and no one would have known. As odorous as he is, though, I doubt Cumberland is a murderer."

"But your brother might be."

Rhuddlan's gaze wandered to Artie, who'd rolled over onto his side. "Yes," he said hoarsely.

"I'm sorry," she said as gently as she could, laying a hand lightly on his arm. The pain of her own family's betrayal stabbed though her heart and nearly brought tears to her eyes despite the passing of the years. Those were the people that were supposed to love you best, and that made their perfidy hurt all the more.

His muscles tensed beneath her fingers but then relaxed, and he covered her hand with his for a moment as he cleared his throat. "Thank you."

There were so many other things Olivia wanted to say, to ask, but the words wouldn't come. Instead she took a slow, deep breath and leaned back against the squabs. If she were lucky, she might be able to sleep a little more this night.

"May I?" Rhuddlan asked, holding out his arm as if to place it around her.

She hesitated. Part of her wanted nothing more than to cuddle up against him and soak up the solace his arms might provide. But part of her was suspicious of what he might want in return, and what he might do if she refused.

"I only wish to allow you some comfort, Miss Stone," he said softly. "Whether or not you avail yourself is entirely your decision."

Her mind held out for just another moment. The duke had kept every promise he'd made her thus far, and had reacted with surprising grace when she broke their kiss earlier in the evening.

"Thank you," she replied in a half-whisper, laying her head on his shoulder. His arm came loosely around her, his hand coming to rest on her elbow.

"I think we both could use all the comfort we can find," he replied, resting his cheek against her hair. "Let's enjoy what we have while we have it."

Olivia's lips curved into a small smile. "I think that's an excellent idea."

Chapter Five

THEY TRAVELED FOR three more days, taking indirect routes, looping around villages whenever possible, and sometimes even doubling back along roads they'd already traversed. His Grace also decided the party would not remain in one place for more than a few hours—long enough to stretch their legs, enjoy a meal, and perhaps wash with a flannel and a basin of clean water.

It was arduous and, in the last day, painful, for Olivia's backside had begun to ache with overuse. On a normal day, she spent a fair amount of time seated while she sewed or embroidered. But there was always something that needed doing or cleaning in her cottage, and she could easily spend half the day or more on her feet. Bumping along in their borrowed carriage for hours and hours on end was harder on her posterior than she'd anticipated. If not for the opportunity to lean into the duke's embrace after Mrs. D. and Miss H. had fallen asleep each night, Olivia was sure she'd be walking oddly when they finally reached their destination.

She was also certain the warmth of him, body and heart, kept her from giving in to the fear that threatened to overwhelm her.

But at last they arrived at Teverton Estate, rumpled and exhausted, as the sun was reaching its peak in the gray sky. They were greeted by Lady Teverton, who explained that her husband was away, but was expecting them and would see them at supper if they were rested enough to dine with him.

Olivia heaved a sigh of relief when she and Artie had been shown to their chamber, closing the door behind her and leaning against it.

"He's not here, Loup," she said, as the dog began his customary inspection. "That means I have time to figure out what to say to him."

Artie gave a single, vague tail-wag in response to her voice, but continued sniffing at the furniture.

"What if he remembers the scandal?" she continued, flattening her palms on the door behind her. She'd had to explain how she was related to Teverton in the letter she'd sent, including her parents' names. "What if he's already made the connection?"

Then a truly awful though barreled into her mind. "What if he tells Rhuddlan?"

It was true that both she and the duke had signed the paper detailing her life interest in her cottage before they left Wales, and that they'd had both her neighbors and two of his secretaries sign as witnesses. Was that agreement still binding even though her name wasn't really Olivia Stone? Would he honor it when he discovered her deception?

A knock on her door jolted her from her musings, and she tried to push her fear away. But when she swung open the door, she once again found the duke on the other side, alone.

"Your Grace..." She gripped the doorknob and tried to focus. "W-what can I do for you?"

"I know this is not exactly proper, Miss Stone, but might I speak with you for a moment? There is something important I'd like to discuss with you."

She swallowed hard, but gestured him inside. "Of course."

He was still dressed in his Cousin Lucas clothing, plain but good quality fabrics that were exquisitely tailored, if wrinkled from traveling. His black hair was a little long, falling over his forehead like a crow's wing, contrasting sharply with his grass green eyes.

Olivia closed the door and clasped her hands together, fighting the urge to brush back his hair. "Would you like to sit?"

He shook his head. "I'd rather stand, actually." His gaze met hers but darted away, and he began pacing. "I have a proposition for you and a confession to make."

"All right," she said, hoping he didn't hear the quaver in her voice. What on earth was he going to say to her? "Which shall we tackle first?"

He stopped and once again met her eyes. "With the confession. You need to know things about me first."

"What things?"

"Society has branded me a monster," he said flatly. "You've likely heard such gossip and rumor in the village."

Olivia nodded slowly, recalling the awful things people had implied about Rhuddlan when she'd inquired.

"It's true that my cousin Rhys went missing during a land dispute...with me," he continued, slowly traversing the room again. "His disappearance has been attributed to me, though I didn't have anything to do with it. My wife's death has also been attributed to me." He paused a moment, pressing his lips together and taking a breath. "She jumped out of a window on the top floor of my home in York, convinced soldiers were coming to kill her. The 'soldiers' were a footman and me, trying to keep her safe from herself."

Olivia dropped into a chair, letting the air *whoosh* out of her lungs. "How awful," she choked out.

"It was." He halted again, and seemed to gather himself. "But there are other things, bad things, that I *did* do. I have ruined people, Miss Stone—financially, socially, and even physically. I employ ruffians and criminals to do these things, and have sometimes done them myself."

"Why?"

The word was barely audible, but he answered firmly. "To keep my people and my interests safe. It sounds trite, I know, but that is my purpose as Duke of Rhuddlan."

She looked up at him from her seat, unsure what to think. "So the ends justify the means."

"Darkness must sometimes be met with darkness."

"Is that how you dealt with Sir George?"

His eyes slid away from hers and one dark eyebrow quirked up. "Yes." When she didn't reply right away, he continued, "I did what was necessary."

"What was necessary?" she asked, clutching the edge of her chair. "What did it take to make Sir George leave me alone?"

"I threatened to kill him and hide his body," Rhuddlan said slowly.

She suppressed a shudder. Olivia had no doubt that it took that much potential violence to deter George Grayson, but the idea of it unsettled her. "And because of your wife and your cousin, he believed you."

"Yes."

Would he follow through on his threat if Sir George returned to his old ways? She shook her head slightly, not wanting to know the answer. "Why tell me this?"

"I want you to have all the facts when you consider my proposal." He sat down in the chair beside her and reached for her hand, clasping it in both of his. "If you are amenable, I think we should be wed."

"Wh-what?"

"There are only two ways to ensure my brother does not succeed me as duke, and the most pleasant is to father an heir."

He said it so matter-of-factly that, for a moment, Olivia found herself nodding along. Of course having a legitimate son would solve one of his problems, but getting that son was a rather intimate affair. And birthing him wouldn't put His Grace in peril.

"And marriage to me would ensure that George Grayson never bothered you again."

She straightened a little more in her chair. Threatening his life might have put Sir George off his pursuit of Olivia, but it very well could have made him even more determined to have her.

But then, marriage to the Duke of Rhuddlan might also make her a target of Lord Nicholas.

"I-I can't," she said, shaking her head. And not just because of his brother—Rhuddlan didn't know who she really was, what she had done. Even if he wasn't bothered by her past or her attempt to hide her identity, Society certainly would be. And so would her victim's family.

"I know it's a lot to take in," he said softly, shifting her hand in his grip. "Particularly after my revelation. I simply thought that, since we seem to get along rather well, we might help solve each other's problems. We might also give each other some pleasure in life, something to look forward to each day. In any case, I'd like you to at least think it over. Wait until you meet your cousin and sort out your situation with him."

She must have looked confused or overwhelmed—she certainly *felt* confused and overwhelmed—for he patted her hand and released it. "It would obviously please me if you accepted, but I don't want you to feel as if I've backed you into a corner. Whatever your answer, our agreement regarding your cottage and protection from Grayson stands."

She nodded dumbly and stood when he stood, watching him cross the chamber and let himself out.

When he'd shut the door behind him, she dropped back into her chair like a sack of rocks falling from the sky. He wanted to marry her?

He wanted to marry her!

And he wanted her to make an informed decision, so he told her about the unsavory ways he sometimes took care of things.

Olivia's head dropped into her hands. She didn't know whether to laugh or cry or howl at the moon when it rose. What in the devil's name was she going to tell him?

Another knock on her door had her on her feet in a flash.

"Teverton's come home early," Mrs. D. said, poking her head in, "and wants to meet you."

Devil take him! Couldn't he wait just a few more minutes so Olivia could untangle her thoughts?

"Am I to meet him in the drawing room or his study?"

"The drawing room," Mrs. D. replied. "We're all to gather there in a quarter of an hour."

Olivia felt her whole body tense. Her entire world would come crashing down in just fifteen minutes' time.

When Rhuddlan entered the drawing room, nearly everyone was already assembled. Miss Stone's two neighbors sat with Teverton's mother, while the viscount himself stood beside his wife, who was staring unhappily at the door.

Rhuddlan reached inside his tailcoat briefly to touch the two letters that had been delivered to Teverton Estate for him from Wales before his arrival. One brought disturbing news, but the other contained the possibility of reinforcements in the battle against Nick. He also surreptitiously checked his pocket watch for the time. If he were to act on the second, more hopeful letter, he would need to make his exit soon. Had Teverton not returned home earlier than scheduled and called his guests to the drawing room,

Rhuddlan would likely be riding away down the road already.

He heard the soft rustle of fabric behind him and turned to see Miss Stone hesitating just inside the door, as if she was suddenly taken with the notion to bolt back up to her chamber. Rhuddlan went to her, struck by the change in her appearance compared to the first time she appeared in his study. She was dressed in his housekeeper's best gown, a frothy sea green frock that Miss Stone must have worked magic on with her needle, for she looked as if she'd belong in any aristocrat's drawing room as an equal and not at all like his housekeeper on her way to Sunday services.

Though she was still akin to the quivering, fearful woman who'd begged for his help.

"Are you nervous?" Rhuddlan asked quietly as he bowed slightly over her hand, remembering keenly the trepidation he'd felt the first time he attended a gathering as the duke.

"Yes," she said, nearly stumbling over the word.

"No matter what happens here, our agreement for your cottage and protection from Grayson is binding," he replied, hoping to reassure her. Perhaps if she was less worried about other things, she would be able to steady herself a bit. "You will always have your home and your safety."

She blanched, and for a moment he thought she might be sick. But she inhaled slowly, then sighed. "Thank you."

"Are you ready to meet your cousin?"

"Yes," she said again, this time with more resolve.

Rhuddlan offered her his arm and led her across the room, giving her a little smile. "Miss Stone, may I present Titus, Lord Teverton."

His lordship also bowed over her hand. "It's a pleasure to meet you, Cousin. I'm only sorry that unfortunate circumstances are what brought you to my attention."

Lady Teverton snorted. "Why do you think she's here?" Rhuddlan arched an eyebrow at her, but Lady Teverton ignored him. "You don't even know if she's truly your cousin."

Miss Stone gasped and Teverton put a hand to his wife's arm. "We talked about this," he said quietly. "Her father is my mother's fourth cousin. The relationship is distant and it took some doing to verify it, but it's there."

"Yes," Lady Teverton replied, not bothering to match her husband's more polite volume. "But you said her father was called Arthur Lockwood. Why is His Grace calling her Miss Stone?"

Miss Stone seemed to wilt like a flower left too long in the sun. "I can explain…"

Rhuddlan's brows drew down over his eyes and his mouth pulled into a frown. Certainly it was out of the ordinary for an unmarried daughter to have a different surname from her father, but there were also plenty of reasonable explanations for such a difference. Why did she look so frightened?

"I'm not really a Stone," she said, her voice barely audible. "My name is Olivia Lockwood, like my father."

"Why not simply use his name, then? Where did Stone come from?" Teverton glanced at his mother, who looked as puzzled as he did.

"I– I began using Stone after my mother died," she said, her eyes darting from Teverton to Mrs. Davies and Miss Hatch, then back again. "I needed to put some, erm, distance between my family and me."

"Distance?" Lady Teverton asked. "What on earth did your family do that you didn't want to be associated with?"

If it was possible, Miss Stone—Lockwood?—paled further. Rhuddlan wanted to reach for her, to comfort her, but he also wanted to know what in blazes was going on. It appeared that the woman he'd so recently proposed marriage to had been living under an assumed name and hadn't told him a thing about it.

"It wasn't what they did, but more what I became known for." Miss Stone looked over at Mrs. Davies and Miss Hatch again, her whole expression mournful, as if she'd killed someone dear to them.

"What you became known for?" Teverton asked, appearing to be as confused as Rhuddlan was.

It was Lady Teverton who made the connection. Her eyes widened and her mouth formed a shape somewhere between an O and a smile. "You're the Olivia Lockwood who was betrothed to the Earl of Windermere's heir some years ago, aren't you?"

Miss Stone's shoulders slumped. "Yes."

"The Olivia Lockwood who was then compromised just days before her wedding?" Lady Teverton pressed.

"Yes," Miss Stone said, lifting her chin and looking Teverton in the eye. "I meant to tell you sooner, my lord, but I didn't know how."

Lady Teverton's nostrils flared. "You must turn her away, Teverton. If anyone finds out she was here, that she's related to you, she could ruin our daughters before we even have any."

What were they on about? Rhuddlan found himself searching the faces of each person in the room, but to no avail.

Teverton looked at his mother again, whose confusion had been supplanted by wide-eyed recognition, then back at Miss Stone. "I can certainly understand that," the viscount said slowly. "Though it would have been nice to know that your reputation is the reason you're having difficulties."

"Would someone please explain what is going on?" Rhuddlan asked, his eyes darting from Teverton to his wife to Miss Stone. But whatever courage Miss Stone had summoned seemed to have faded, and her gaze dropped to Teverton's shoes.

"Miss Olivia Lockwood was the daughter of a wealthy merchant—Teverton's distant cousin—and became betrothed to the Earl of Windermere's heir." Lady Teverton's smile was almost smug as she recounted the story. "But she was ruined right before her wedding. She was caught in an intimate embrace with a footman and abandoned by her fiancé."

Rhuddlan's first thought was that someone should have called out old Windy's heir. No gentleman would ever jilt a lady, no matter the circumstances. Once he'd given his word, he was bound to follow through.

His mind let that go for a moment and seized on two other, brand new facts: Miss Stone was in fact a gentleman's daughter, not the lowborn laborer he'd assumed her to be, and she'd been ruined by a footman.

Miss Stone's mouth was set in a hard line, face burning red. "I was afraid you wouldn't see me if you knew."

"You're right about that," Lady Teverton answered for her husband. "You deserve whatever fate has dealt you after what you did."

Then the mantle clock struck the hour.

Rhuddlan stared at it dumbly for a moment, fishing out his gold pocket watch and comparing it to the clock atop the fireplace. "I'm afraid I must go," he said, his voice sounding stilted to his ears. "I have an appointment that I cannot miss."

Miss Stone made a strangled, gasping noise, then bolted from the room. Rhuddlan wanted to go after her —question after question filled his head—but he could not miss the opportunity to join forces with a man even more powerful than he was. It might be his only chance to bring his brother to heel.

He said his hurried good-byes to the rest of the assemblage and made his way out to the stables. When he reached the entryway he paused, glancing up the staircase in the direction of Miss Stone's chamber. Even if he had the time, she likely wouldn't welcome visitors now, anyway. Perhaps, if he wasn't too late getting back, he could speak with her then and get answers to some of his questions.

Perhaps, by then, he might work out how he felt about her deception.

One of the letters sent to Teverton Estate for Rhuddlan had been from the Duke of Sussex, who Rhuddlan had known well for a number of years. Sussex's letter directed Rhuddlan to meet him at what turned out to be a small farmhouse, with no signs of life except the single cow grazing in the pasture.

Rhuddlan stabled his horse and walked cautiously up to the house, circling the structure before trying the front door. It was unlocked so he entered slowly, sweeping his eyes around each room as he moved through the ground floor.

"Ah, there you are," came a voice from what seemed to be a small parlor, the door standing open. Prince Augusts Frederick, Duke of Sussex sat in a crude wooden chair by the fireplace, his feet propped up on the cold grate.

"I made sure I wasn't followed," Rhuddlan replied, dropping into a matching chair opposite his friend's.

"Good." Sussex sighed. "You heard Cumberland is back in the country?"

Rhuddlan nodded. He'd had a letter from Lewis in the packet, too, containing reports from more than one of Rhuddlan's informants who'd spotted Cumberland. "Without his wife and child."

Sussex pooched his lips out. "He apparently stopped overnight at my old hunting lodge, and caught the housekeeper and butler by surprise. They wrote to gently rebuke me for not letting them know he was coming. But he hasn't written to the family to say he was here."

That was tantamount to sneaking into the country. "My informants say he's been seen in St. Asaph."

"That's bold," Cumberland said, his brows rising. St. Asaph was only a few scant miles from Rhuddlan Hall. "Consorting with Nick?"

Rhuddlan shook his head, stretching his legs out before him. "They wouldn't be so careless. I'm surprised Cumberland is even in Wales while Nick is there."

"Where is Lord Nicholas?"

Rhuddlan lolled his head back. "Last report I had said he was in Shrewsbury." Far enough away to not be personally responsible for anything happening at Rhuddlan Hall, but close enough to direct his minions.

"Any other disturbances since the mill?"

Rhuddlan briefly described his own injury and the attack on Vaughn. "Neither attack can be traced back to our esteemed brothers, of course, but Vaughn's beating was certainly a result of his employment with me."

Sussex sighed, clasping his hands together in his lap. "What can I do, Rhuddlan?"

"The biggest help would be information—whatever your people find out about Cumberland, about Nick, about anything they might be doing." Rhuddlan's network of domestic spies was as wide as he'd implied it was to George Grayson, but they couldn't be everywhere at once.

"I will instruct them to send copies of any pertinent information directly to you, as well as to me," Sussex said agreeably.

"Excellent. Perhaps between the two of us, we'll be able to put together a case against at least one of them," Rhuddlan replied.

Sussex's eyes went wide. "You intend to prosecute?"

"I highly doubt anything would come of a prosecution against Cumberland, even if I had solid evidence," Rhuddlan said, sitting up straighter in his chair. "Even if he were convicted of something, he'd claim Privilege of Peerage and would not be punished."

Sussex seemed to relax slightly at that pronouncement, but still looked worried. "But you would pursue charges against your own brother?"

Rhuddlan understood his friend's concern. Nearly everything Nick might conceivably be charged with would result in a sentence of hanging if he were found guilty. And, as he was not yet Duke of Rhuddlan, Nick would not be able to claim Privilege of Peerage like his patron. "I'd rather it not come to that, but Nick has destroyed people's lives. And the destruction has become worse since I left Rhuddlan Hall."

He pulled from his waistcoat pocket one of the letters he'd taken from his chamber at Teverton Estate and handed it to Sussex. It was from his temporary principle secretary, detailing two more attacks that took place on the grounds of the estate and a parish church nearby set afire while people were inside.

Sussex's eyes widened once more, but when he looked up he was shaking his head. "You can't know it was Cumberland and Lord Nicholas who did this."

Rhuddlan pulled one more, smaller note from his pocket and handed it over. The note was unsigned and in someone else's hand, but there was no mistaking who was behind it.

Turn over control of the dukedom to your brother, Luca, or the violence against your people will continue.

"This still doesn't prove it was him," Sussex said weakly. "It could be someone working on his behalf."

It most definitely was someone working on Nick's behalf, and profiting from it. But Rhuddlan didn't say so aloud. "Look at my name, Sussex. Who in the world ever called me Luca?"

Sussex stared at the note for several long moments. "Your mother," he said softly.

Rhuddlan's mother had been a Moldovian noblewoman, and had affectionately called her younger sons by the Romanian forms of their names. Nick had been Nicu since his birth, and Rhuddlan had been Luca. A lump formed in his throat at the thought— Maria, Duchess of Rhuddlan had died when her middle son was only sixteen and her youngest just seven years old.

Rhuddlan cleared his throat. "This is most certainly Nick's doing."

Sussex looked up from the note. "He's invoked your mother's memory and threatened thousands of people in the same ransom demand. Has he no conscience?"

"Perhaps he's hoping the threat will be enough to scare me into compliance," Rhuddlan said, slouching down in his chair again. "But I want to be prepared in case he thinks to follow through on it."

"Of course."

He said it with a measure of conviction, but Rhuddlan could hear the doubt lingering in his voice. Who could blame him, though? What other man would plainly state his intention to potentially see his brother executed?

Rhuddlan rose, offering his hand. "Thank you, Sussex. Truly. I know this can't be easy for you, either."

Sussex stood, too, and shook Rhuddlan's hand. "We must do what we can to keep people safe, though, mustn't we?"

"That is our responsibility."

Rhuddlan left the farmhouse and saddled his horse. Sussex must surely think him a monster, but at least the man had pledged his assistance. If he was going to bring Nick to heel and have any hope of reining in Cumberland, he was going to need all the help he could get.

Chapter Six

For the third time in a fortnight, Olivia found herself ushered into an aristocrat's study. Lord Teverton had thought it prudent to convene there and talk over her situation, and Olivia agreed—she certainly didn't want to have that discussion in front of everyone.

The curtains were wide open, allowing sunlight to illuminate every corner of the room. There were papers and books on most flat surfaces, save the floor, as if his lordship spent a good deal of time working there.

Lord Teverton gestured to a chair near the fireplace. "Would you like to sit?"

Olivia nodded and perched on the edge of the chair while her cousin made himself comfortable opposite her.

"Where would you like to begin?" he asked, crossing one leg over the other knee.

An excellent question, and one that she couldn't answer. This man might be her nearest relation, but she didn't know him. She shrugged her shoulders in response. "What would you like to know?"

"You said in your letter that you were in a difficult situation. Would you tell me about that?"

She reached back in her mind, trying to remember what she'd written in the letter that had accompanied Rhuddlan's. "The bare facts are simple: my income is declining, and I can no longer support myself. My only options were to appeal to you or to wed a man who was blackmailing me."

"Blackmailing you?" Lord Teverton asked. He sounded as if he was trying to keep his tone casual, but didn't quite do it.

"He knows my real identity," she said with a frown. "I went to Wales to escape Miss Olivia Lockwood, to live a quiet life. But this man knew my parents and figured out who I was."

"And he tried to coerce you into marriage."

She nodded. "He thinks himself rather grand and wanted a connection to an aristocrat, no matter how distant."

"Ah." Lord Teverton's posture relaxed a bit. "That is a concept I am familiar with. But I take it you don't want this match."

Olivia shuddered at the thought of being shackled to Sir George. Would Rhuddlan keep his promise and provide her protection now that he knew she'd lied about her identity? "If he is left to his own devices, he will kill me, my lord."

The corners of Lord Teverton's mouth turned up. "You could just say you don't want to wed him."

"You think I'm exaggerating," she replied, feeling the heat creep into her cheeks.

"You are not the first lady to consider wedding a less than perfect suitor," he said gently. "If it's a dowry you need—"

"He will kill me," she said through clenched teeth. "He has described to me how he will do it."

The shock on Lord Teverton's face was almost gratifying. "You're serious."

Olivia tried to relax her jaw. Being brushed off was not new—only Mrs. D., Miss H., and Rhuddlan had believed her when she'd first told them about Sir George's threats, and no one had listened about the footman—but it still stung. "I am."

"And both your parents have gone on to their reward." Lord Teverton leaned back in his chair and blew out a breath. "No wonder you asked for my help."

"There's one more thing, my lord," she said hesitantly, clasping her hands together in her lap. Would he believe her this time? Or would he think she was trying to squeeze more money out of him? "When my father died, he left a sizable sum to my mother. But she spent every shilling, then began making purchases on credit she could never hope to repay."

His eyes narrowed for a moment. "So when she died, you were left with nothing."

"Nothing but debt." And her ruined reputation, but that betrayal was still too painful to speak of.

Understanding dawned on Lord Teverton's face. "Is that why you ran?"

Olivia nodded, fighting back tears as the fear and desperation of her flight from her childhood home rushed back. "I was alone, with no income and no practical skills except sewing. With the debt and my, erm, infamy hanging over my head, I no one would help me. I sold Mother's jewelry and went as far away as that sum would take me."

He nodded as if he understood. But could a man who had only known plenty truly understand what it was like to have nothing?

"What is it you require of me, then?"

His voice was gentle, but Olivia cringed at his choice of words. "Require" made her feel as though she was forcing him to submit to her. "I just..." She took in a breath and let it out slowly. "I just want to live quietly, my lord. I want to be able to buy bread and pay Artie's dog tax and... and work on my sewing in peace."

"You wish to return to your home in Wales?"

She nodded. "If it's safe to do so."

"I can certainly provide you with an allowance—that should take care of your bread and your dog," Lord Teverton said with a smile. "I don't know what can be done about this Sir George, but perhaps Rhuddlan and I can come up with something if we talk it through together."

"You'll decide my fate together, then?" That bolt of fear and desperation shot through her body again. Would Rhuddlan seek to punish her for hiding her identity from him?

"Oh, we'll not do anything until one of us has spoken to you, of course," he said quickly. "You are the one most impacted by his behavior."

The bolt subsided, but Olivia's heart continued to pound. Her father had always trusted Lord Teverton's father, but could she trust this man? She swallowed hard. "Thank you."

"I will consult my account books and Rhuddlan, then you and I can talk further." He rose, a polite signal that she was being dismissed.

She hesitated, but stood and allowed him to walk her to the door, then made her way up to her chamber where Artie was waiting with his usual wagging tale.

Olivia knelt down and put her arms around him. "We might be able to go home, soon, Loup Garou. We might be able to go home and be safe."

Artie sat down and rested his chin on her shoulder.

"You're a good boy," she said, stroking his soft fur, "and the one good thing that came from this whole mess. If my mother hadn't betrayed me, I would never have run away to Wales, and wouldn't have been next door when Mr. Davies brought you home."

A knock on the door stole Artie's attention away, and he barked at the noise. It was probably just as well —another couple of minutes and she might have been blubbering into his fur.

Mrs. D. was at the door when Olivia opened it, dropping into a curtsy. "Miss Lockwood."

"No, Mrs. D. I'm still the seamstress who lives in the cottage next door to yours."

Mrs. D. met her eyes and offered a small smile. "Do you want to talk about it?"

Olivia didn't want to talk to anyone, possibly ever again, but she owed Mrs. D. an explanation. "Why don't you come in."

Olivia built up the fire and settled in before it with her friend. "It's true that I was the daughter of Arthur Lockwood, and that I was once betrothed. He was a nice, sweet gentleman I met at a soiree during my second season. When my father contracted smallpox and later died from it, my fiancé agreed to postpone the wedding."

"Oh, how sad," Mrs. D. said. She reached out to pat Olivia's hand, but hesitated midway, then pulled her hand back to the arm of her chair.

Olivia pretended not to notice and pushed the hurt from her mind. "We got through it. But then my mother started talking about how lonely she was going to be when I married. She grew despondent whenever someone brought up the wedding, and eventually refused to come out of her bedchamber."

Mrs. D. made some kind of tut-tut noise under her breath, but didn't comment.

"Then one day, she sent me to a bakery near our home in London—she wanted a special kind of biscuit they made there with her tea that day. And she insisted I take a specific footman with me."

At the word "footman," Mrs. D.'s eyes and mouth went round.

Olivia nodded. "Just before we entered the bakery, the footman pulled me against him and kissed me."

Mrs. D. gasped, but Olivia didn't stop.

"There were plenty of witnesses, two of whom were close friends of my mother's who made it a point to tell the story to everyone they knew."

"Oh, dear..."

"My fiancé said he was still willing to go through with the wedding," Olivia continued, trying not to remember the look on his face when he'd confronted her. He'd spoken more about his honor and keeping important promises than about their happiness together. "But it was clear that he didn't believe my denials."

"You didn't marry him, though, did you?"

Olivia shook her head. "I knew he would hold that incident over my head for the rest of our lives, so I cried off." She looked into the flickering fire, unable to make eye contact with the woman who had been her closest friend for years. "The footman disappeared after that, and I found out later that he'd suddenly come into a large sum of money."

"It wasn't—"

"My mother had paid him to ruin me."

"Oh, my sweet girl."

Mrs. D. was up out of her chair with her arms spread, and Olivia stood up to meet her. "She said she couldn't bear to have me leave her," Olivia continued softly, trying to keep the bitterness from her voice that was still present in her heart, even after all the time that had passed. "She died a year later, Mrs. D., and left me with more debt than I could ever hope to pay back."

The tears came then. Olivia hadn't realized how much the old wound still ached, but Mrs. D.'s fierce embrace made her feel safe in a way she hadn't since before her father died. She sobbed into Mrs. D.'s shoulder until her lungs burned and her eyes dried, unable to understand why her own mother would have left her to such a fate.

Rhuddlan paced the length of his bedchamber that night, back and forth, unable to quiet his body or his mind. He'd received a second letter from Lewis describing more violence at Rhuddlan Hall, violence that had not attempted to follow him away from his people as he'd hoped.

He made his way over to one of the windows and leaned his forehead against the cool pane of glass. Between the ugliness pouring in from his home, the time he'd spent considering the potential execution of his own brother, and the revelation of Miss Stone's true identity, it had been a very long day.

"What I need is a book," he said aloud, his breath temporarily clouding the glass. "Something just interesting enough to take my mind off my troubles, but boring enough to put me to sleep."

He pealed himself off the window and headed down the main staircase to Teverton's library, taking a single candle with him to light his way. The large chamber was, as he'd expected at this late hour, devoid of people. The darkness and quiet were a relief—Rhuddlan felt some of the tension in his body bleed away just walking through the door. He chose one of the tall bookshelves at random and began browsing the titles.

A voice startled him in the gloom. "Is that you, Your Grace?"

Miss Stone—he had a hard time thinking of her as Miss Lockwood—stood in the doorway holding her own candle, a large shawl wrapped around what looked to be a nightdress, her bright hair trailing over one shoulder in a thick braid. Her voice was low, reminding him of the late hour and the impropriety of meeting her this way. Was she trying to trap him? To remedy her ruined reputation? He glanced out the open door, but couldn't see much beyond the door frame itself.

"Did I startle you?" she asked quietly.

He shook his head reflexively. "No."

"Good." She started to take a step into the room, then stopped.

"If you're here for a book, don't let me stop you." There was a slightly harsh note in his voice, but he wasn't sure if it was residual anger at his brother or the fact that he felt betrayed by Miss Stone's revelation.

She took a couple of steps then, but went no father. "I– I hadn't meant to do this now, but perhaps we should talk."

"About what?"

"Your proposal of marriage."

His brows rose a fraction—in all the excitement, he'd nearly forgotten the offer he'd made her. Had it been only the day before? "Yes, we should discuss that."

"I–I can't marry you," she said haltingly, pulling her shawl more tightly around her. "And after what you heard about me this afternoon, I doubt very much that you still want to marry me."

Rhuddlan probably should have felt relieved at no longer being tied to such a woman. Instead he felt a prick of disappointment, which confused him even more. "If that's what you think is best."

Her brows drew down over her eyes. "Don't you think it best? Given who I am."

How was he supposed to answer that? He wanted to ask her why she'd lied to him about who she was, but just one word came to his lips. "Quite."

"Good." Her posture relaxed somewhat and she took a step back toward the door. "I should probably return to my chamber, then."

One of them certainly should, but despite his mixed feelings about her, Rhuddlan was rather reluctant to part from her. "It's been— This day has not been kind to me. Will you sit with me for a while?" It was a bold— and entirely inappropriate—request, and he wasn't really sure why he made it.

"You want to sit with me?" There was curiosity in her expression when she turned back to face him, though it was tinged with disbelief.

"Yes," he said, then quickly added, "but if you would rather leave, I won't stop you."

She tilted her head slightly to one side, appraising him, and he crossed his arms over his chest as if to cover himself. He'd discarded his tailcoat shortly after returning from his clandestine meeting at the farmhouse and rolled his shirtsleeves up to his elbows —decidedly inappropriate dress in the presence of a lady. Even if the lady in question was in her nightdress.

"The day has not been kind to you, either," he continued softly. "I suspect you might be in need of comfort as badly as I am."

That must have struck a chord. Her posture, her shoulders, even the set of her mouth relaxed a little. "That's true enough. What did you have in mind?"

"Anything that will bring us both pleasure," he responded. When she lifted an eyebrow at him, he smiled for the first time that night. "There are few things I'd like more than to take you to bed, Miss Stone, but that's not what I meant."

"I'm not Miss Stone, Your Grace," she said tightly, turning away again.

"My apologies. That's a habit I have yet to break." He took a step toward her, suppressing the urge to reach out and touch her. "What if we dispense with formality when we're alone? May I call you Olivia?"

She turned back at the sound of her name on his lips. "And what would I call you?"

"Rhuddlan," he answered automatically. "Or Lucas, if you'd like."

"Lucas," she said softly, coming closer to him, "the man who held me in the carriage as we ran from danger."

"That was pleasurable, was it not?"

She nodded, stopping inches from him and stroking her thumb over his cheek. "It was for me."

"For me, too." Her thumb traced the corner of his mouth and his heart kicked into a gallop. "We could try that again."

She didn't move for a long moment, then she let the shawl slip to the floor and slid her arms around his shoulders. "Like this?"

"Yes," he murmured, drawing her against him. Her body was warm, separated from his in some places by only her nightdress. When she sighed into the crook of his neck, he nearly came undone. "I would like very much to kiss you, Olivia," he whispered in her ear.

She stiffened in his arms, but only for a moment. "I would like that, too."

Her mouth was open and waiting for him when his lips found hers. He captured first her top lip, then the bottom one, before covering her mouth with his and sliding his tongue inside.

When she moaned softly and combed her fingers through his hair, he grinned. "Did you like that?"

"Yes," she murmured, her eyes opening to meet his in the firelight. "Shall we do it again?"

He arched an eyebrow and bent his head, kissing her more deeply this time, sliding one hand down her back to cup her derriere. She pressed her breasts against his chest in response, slipping a hand inside his collar.

"You feel so good," he mumbled, trailing kisses down her neck. She froze and he lifted his head. "Olivia?"

She pulled away, picking her shawl up from the floor and gathering it around her. "I'm sorry—"

Her voice caught on the word, and he wanted to take her in his arms again, to kiss away whatever had caused her distress. Instead, he let her put as much distance between them as she felt was necessary.

"No apology required," he said gently. "Remember?"

He thought he saw the corners of her mouth turn up slightly, but he couldn't be sure in the low light.

"I remember." She adjusted the shawl, pulling it up over her shoulders. "But I'm still sorry."

"Do you want to leave?"

"No, but I probably should." Was that reluctance in her voice?

She was right, reluctance or no. She should leave and so should he. He should return to his own chamber so he could finish himself off and try to get some sleep. He would need to keep his head clear if he hoped to deal with Nick and Cumberland effectively.

But neither of them moved.

"Could we... could we actually sit for a while?" she asked, gesturing to the sofa that sat near the door.

"Certainly."

She shut the door behind her before seating herself on the sofa, setting her candle on a side table. Rhuddlan joined her, feeling rather awkward about it. Only moments ago they'd been in a heated embrace that might have been heading toward the removal of clothing. How were they to conduct themselves now?

He decided to take his cue from Olivia. Taking a seat beside her, he smiled when she inched closer and took her hand in his.

Then the words came. "Why didn't you tell me who you were?" he asked quietly.

"I couldn't," she answered, casting her eyes down toward their joined hands. "After my mother and fiancé, then Sir George... I didn't know who to trust."

"Your—what?" He knew about her problems with Grayson, of course, but what was this about her mother and fiancé?

She squeezed his hand and haltingly told him about her betrothal, her father's death, and a horrifying agreement made between her mother and a footman.

"Oh, God, Olivia, I'm so sorry." He felt helpless, sitting there on the sofa unable to do anything more than hold her hand while she explained how her own family had betrayed her.

"I couldn't risk you recognizing my real name and refusing to help me," she said in a thick voice. "I needed your help too badly."

"I understand," he said, shifting closer to her to wrap her in his arms.

She relaxed against him, sighing into his shoulder, and he caught the scent of vanilla on her skin. They sat there together, holding one another, until the clock on the mantle struck one before reluctantly parting.

They crept up the stairs to their own chambers, her arm threaded through his. When they reached her door, she paused. "Good night, Rhuddlan...Lucas," she whispered, caressing his stubbly cheek.

He lifted their clasped hands to his lips and kissed hers. "Good night, Olivia."

He waited for her to go inside, then took himself to his own chamber where he shed his clothing and fell into bed.

Rhuddlan awoke the next morning feeling more relaxed than he had in days. He even found himself smiling as he made his way down to the dining room for breakfast. But no sooner had he pushed open the dining room door, than Miss Hatch burst in with wild eyes.

"He found her."

"Who found whom?" Teverton asked, but Rhuddlan already knew the answer.

"George Grayson is here, and he's found Olivia."

Chapter Seven

"Where are you going?"

Teverton's voice carried across the dining room, but Rhuddlan didn't stop. "To do something stupid."

He banged through the door, towing Miss Hatch with him. "Where are they?"

"She took Artie for a walk toward the home farm," Miss Hatch told him, running with him to the front entrance and pointing. "That way."

"Thank you," he said, and made a dash for the door. His blood was already pounding through his veins, his muscles taut and ready for action. He took off across the manicured lawn, running at top speed in seconds, hoping there was a horse already saddled when he got to the stables.

He had to get to Olivia before Grayson hurt her.

There was a horse in the process of being saddled when he burst through the stable door. Apparently Teverton had planned to go riding after breakfast but Rhuddlan commandeered the beast, calling to the stable hands to take it up with their master.

He mounted the horse and turned it quickly, cheered momentarily by the responsiveness of the animal. When he gave the command the sleek Thoroughbred bolted out of the stable, practically flying as it drove toward the home farm.

"Oh, good boy!" Rhuddlan shouted over the wind rushing past, crouching low over the horse's neck. "Let's go find her."

Halfway to the home farm Rhuddlan slowed the horse to a quick trot, even though every ounce of his being screamed for him to ride faster. He scanned the horizon in every direction, looking for a flash of color, listening for a cry for help.

That's when he heard barking.

He slowed the horse again, searching frantically for the source of the sound. Then he saw them, a hundred yards away: a man and a woman facing each other, with a hellbeast between them.

Rhuddlan dismounted, keeping his eyes on the tableau as he quietly tied the horse to an old fence post and crept closer. Suppressing his body's urge to charge in headlong, he tried to recall his days as a scout in the Army. Sneaking into enemy territory had been his specialty.

He skirted the edge of the scene, trying to get far enough behind the man to escape his peripheral vision. As Rhuddlan drew closer, he could see the man—by now he could identify George Grayson's pig-like face—held a pistol, and was alternately pointing it at the woman and the beast. The beast was Artie, as he'd suspected, in full battle posture: he stood in a half-crouch ready to pounce, ears pinned back against his skull, teeth bared, fur standing on end all the way down his spine. Every time Grayson so much as flinched, Artie launched into a tirade of vicious barking, keeping himself positioned between his mistress and the threat.

Good dog.

"Please, Sir George, I'll do anything you want. Just
— *Please*, don't hurt Artie."

Grayson laughed and Artie lunged, not far enough
to engage his threat but enough to make the man
freeze. Olivia's eyes flicked to the side of Grayson for a
split second, and Rhuddlan knew she'd seen him.
Good. Perhaps he could warn her before he began his
charge.

"You'll do what I want, all right." Grayson's words
rang out clearly over the empty meadow they stood in.
"You'll watch your precious mongrel perish. Then you'll
join him. No one threatens me and gets away with it."

Rhuddlan ran the remaining distance, tackling
Grayson from behind and pinning him to the ground.

Olivia screamed as Artie sprung, unleashing his
inner war dog and latching himself to Grayson's arm.
Grayson screamed, too, when Artie's teeth pierced flesh
and the dog began to shake his prey. The knight
released the pistol and tried to pull away from his
captors, but neither Rhuddlan nor Artie was ready to
let him go.

"Olivia, love, come get this pistol," Rhuddlan said
with forced calm, driving his knee into Grayson's back.
"Old George here won't be needing it any more."

There were streaks of blood on the sleeve of
Grayson's tailcoat now, and Artie's growling had grown
more intense. "You let him go now, Loup Garou,"
Rhuddlan said to the dog. "I'll take it from here."

"*Loup! Lâcher!*" Olivia commanded in a shaky voice
as she came closer. Artie looked her in the eye as if to
acknowledge the order, but refused to release his hold.
"Loup Garou, I am safe now," she said gently, picking

up the pistol with one trembling hand and stroking the dog's fur with the other. "You've done your job. *Lâcher, s'il vous plaît.*"

Artie finally relented, and Rhuddlan felt the breath go out of Grayson in a heaving sigh.

"Take him and Teverton's horse," Rhuddlan gestured in the direction of the Thoroughbred some distance away, "and go back to the house." Her brows rose nearly to her sunlit hair and Rhuddlan nodded. "I would like to have a word with Sir George alone."

If she knew what he was planning, she didn't indicate her feeling about it. She simply met his gaze and nodded slightly, grasping Artie's collar and leading him away. Rhuddlan waited until she'd untied the horse and headed across the meadow with her little menagerie, then flipped Grayson over beneath him.

The knight was smiling. "Are you going to kill me now?"

Rhuddlan's fist crashed into the man's face without warning, producing a dull *thud*. "I said I would." *Thud.* "I told you that if you ever came near her again I'd come after you, and no one would ever find you." *Thud.*

Rhuddlan stood and hauled Grayson to his feet by the lapels of his coat, then threw him back to the ground. "Do you know what they called me in the Army? What Polite Society calls me now?"

He kicked Grayson in the ribs, watching with satisfaction as the man turned onto his side and curled up. "They call me Devil, George Grayson. And you should be afraid."

Grayson tucked his head and covered it with one arm. "Please..." he croaked.

"Oh, you want me to have mercy on you?" Rhuddlan bellowed, turning Grayson onto his back once again. "You want me to show you the mercy you didn't show Olivia Stone?"

"She's not... who she says... she is..."

"I know exactly who she is, you worthless maggot." Rhuddlan brought his boot down on Grayson's groin. The knight tried to bring his knees up, but Rhuddlan didn't move. "From this moment, she is her own woman. Do you understand?"

Grayson nodded faintly.

"She says she never wants to see hide nor hair of you again." Rhuddlan put a little more pressure on Grayson's groin. "You will not speak to her, nor about her, ever again."

Grayson attempted another nod, but looked as if he was going to be sick and couldn't manage it.

"You will not go within three miles of her, her home, her dog, or anyone she interacts with." Rhuddlan removed his boot from Grayson's groin, and bent low over him. "And if I find out you even thought about her, I'll hunt you down and finish what I started here."

Rhuddlan reached out and patted his adversary's cheek, chuckling when the man flinched.

He straightened, smoothing out his wrinkled coat and waistcoat as he walked away. For a brief moment, he truly had wanted to kill George Grayson. The man was no better than excrement clinging to the bottom of Rhuddlan's boot, the way he terrorized people who had no recourse against him.

But a violent death would only bring trouble for Teverton, and likely for Olivia, too, once the victim was identified. Rhuddlan didn't want to be responsible for bringing that upon them, nor for adding another death to the tally his conscience already agonized over. Besides, there were other ways to punish a man who valued money and status above all else.

He trudged slowly through the meadow, lifting his face to the bright sun that shone down on him. There could not be light without darkness, and Olivia was surely the light of his life.

He was certainly the darkness in hers.

By the time he reached the house his body had calmed somewhat, but his mind was still churning. He went straight to his chamber to clean up, having found some of Grayson's blood splattered on his sleeves, and to scribble down a few notes regarding further action he wished to take against the worm.

When he was presentable once again, he went looking for Olivia. He found her in the stable, arms around her knees in the back of an empty stall with Artie lying against her. Her body visibly shook, but she was quiet and her eyes were dry.

"Olivia?"

Her lids lifted and her eyes met his. "Is he dead?"

"No." Not yet, anyway. It was still possible for Grayson to die of his injuries, particularly if he couldn't get himself out of that meadow.

She nodded, resting her chin on her knees, but didn't speak.

Rhuddlan took a few steps into the stall and crouched down. "Did you want him to be?"

"Yes," she said fiercely. Then, "No. I don't know."

"I didn't kill him," Rhuddlan said with as much gentleness as he could muster. "But you will never have to worry about him again. You, your neighbors, Artie...you're safe again."

"You're certain?"

"I'm certain."

She held his gaze for several moments, then sniffled and buried her face in her arms. Rhuddlan strode over to her and sat beside her. He didn't speak or touch her. He only wanted her to know that he was there should she need him.

After a moment, she laid her head on his shoulder. "Thank you. I wish it hadn't come to this, but I'm glad you were here when it did."

He rested his head against hers. "I promised you I'd keep you safe."

"You've done that better than my own family."

"Did things go badly with Teverton?" Rhuddlan felt his hands curling into fists.

She shook her head, tickling his cheek with her hair. "No, he was fair and rather compassionate."

And old wound then. His hands were aching from their repeated blows against Grayson's skull, and his heart joined them.

"My mother," she said in a near whisper. "I know it was years ago, but it still hurts."

"I know." He thought of Nick, of their former closeness, and of what their relationship had become. "Your family are supposed to be the people you trust the most, but too often they're the ones who hurt you the most instead."

"Too bad we can't choose our family," she said with a wistful note in her voice.

He started to agree—it would have been an enormous relief to be able to choose his heir, after all—then stopped. "We can, to an extent."

She sat up to look at him. "What do you mean?"

He hoped the disappointment at the loss of her touch didn't show on his face. "You are the perfect example—you've got Mrs. Davies and Miss Hatch."

"My surrogate mothers," she smiled. "Especially Mrs. D. She took me as her own the day I took up residence in the cottage next door to hers. I wouldn't have Artie if not for her and her husband."

He couldn't help but return her smile. "As I said."

"What about you?" she asked, settling against him again, with her head on his shoulder. "Who is your chosen family?"

You. The word came unbidden to his mind, but he refrained from saying it aloud. Was it really true? Or did he simply wish it to be? "I suppose I don't really have any."

She touched her forehead to the crook of his neck in a gesture that felt awfully similar to being nuzzled. "No one?" she asked softly. "Everyone should have at least one person in this world they can trust."

He set his arm about her, letting his hand come to rest on her shoulder. "Yes, they should."

Olivia elected to remain in her chamber for the rest of the day with the exception of Artie's walks, and she took either Mrs. D. or Miss H. with her then, staying close to the house. She just couldn't bring herself to smile and answer the multitude of questions she knew they would all have as if they were gossiping about who danced with whom at last night's ball. If Rhuddlan had come upon her only a minute later, she and Artie might well have been dead.

The next morning, though, she forced herself to walk down to the dining room for breakfast. She had lived on her own for years, had survived her father's death and her mother's betrayal. She could certainly survive breakfast with her family and closest friends.

To her great relief, no one made a fuss when she entered the dining room. Mrs. D. and Miss H. were already at the table with Lord Teverton, and Rhuddlan was perusing the variety of dishes on the sideboard. Lord Teverton's wife and mother were not present—another relief.

She smiled at Rhuddlan, feeling suddenly shy as she approached the sideboard.

He gave her a small smile in return. "How do you feel this morning?" he asked in a near whisper.

"I have had better days," she answered quietly, "but I'll do."

"Good."

She'd hoped he would touch her, even just fingertips on her shoulder, but he didn't. And he was right not to, she reminded herself. There were rules to follow in polite company, and breaking them could lead to some very unpleasant consequences.

Olivia added some eggs to her plate and a triangle of toast, then found a place at the table, making sure to meet everyone's gaze at least once before she began eating.

She'd just mentally congratulated herself for making a good start when Rhuddlan said between bites, "I think it best if I return to Rhuddlan Hall as soon as possible, Teverton. Your hospitality has been wonderful, but I have business to attend to at home before I return to London."

Teverton undoubtedly answered, but Olivia didn't hear it. Rhuddlan was going back? What did that mean for her? For them?

"Miss Sto— Miss Lockwood, if you'd like to return at this time I would be happy to escort you and your companions."

She stared at Rhuddlan for a moment before his words registered, opening her mouth to speak but having no idea how to answer him.

Lord Teverton took the opportunity to interject. "You and I can conclude our business after breakfast, Cousin."

With both her finances and physical safety secured, there would be nothing keeping her at Teverton Estate. She could return to her home, her customers, her neighbors... If she even had a home. She'd signed Rhuddlan's documents under a false name, and Michaelmas—the next quarter day, when rent would be due—was fast approaching.

"Thank you, my lord. I believe that's a good idea." She turned to Rhuddlan, seated across the table and one place to the left of her. "Might you have a moment for me this afternoon, Your Grace?"

He looked slightly startled, but nodded. "Certainly."

Excellent. She could get her affairs in order, then decide what to do with herself. Mrs. D. and Miss H. could travel home with Rhuddlan either way, and return to their own lives. Even without having made the decision yet, merely having a plan gave Olivia's confidence a boost.

Lord Teverton waited until she'd finished eating then walked with her to his study, where they sat in the same places they'd occupied only two days ago.

No sooner than he sat down, did Lord Teverton pop back up and fetch something from his desk. "I wish I could offer you more," he said, holding out a piece of paper to her when he returned to his seat. "But you are such a distant relation..."

"Nor am I the daughter of anyone important," she concluded for him.

"Your father was a gentleman, and that makes you a lady," he responded. "But no, he was not of the *ton*, if that's what you mean."

Olivia unfolded the paper and saw a sum printed there that would defray the cost of all her needs except the rent for her cottage. And if her few remaining customers decided to continue patronizing her, she might even be able to begin hosting Mrs. D. and Miss H for dinner.

"This is more than generous, my lord," she said after being silent for too long. "Truthfully, I was not expecting such a number." Then she hurried to add, "I didn't know what to expect from you, to be completely honest."

"I didn't know what to expect from you, either, when I received your letter," he said, resting his hand on the arm of his chair. "As you know, my wife was convinced you were trying to swindle me by falsely claiming to be a cousin. But I can see your father in you when you speak, and particularly when you talk to that dog of yours. As soon as you admitted your real name, I knew you were Arthur's daughter."

Olivia smiled at that. She and her father hadn't had much in common when he was alive, or so she had believed. Maybe they had been more alike than she realized. "Did you know him well?"

"We were not close, but I did see him once or twice a year when he went to Town for the Season with you and your mother." Lord Teverton broke into a grin. "He had an old hound that he took with him everywhere, much to your mother's dismay."

"Rex!" she exclaimed. "I remember him—on the occasions Papa did leave him at home, it took two footmen to hold him back, and he'd make such a fuss trying to follow Papa out the door."

"Like father, like daughter," Lord Teverton said, giving her a there-you-have-it gesture with one hand.

"Thank you, my lord," she replied, her smile gentling. "Not just for the financial assistance, but for reserving your judgment of me. And for the memory of Papa and Rex—I hadn't thought of them together for many years now."

"Happy to be of service," he said with a smile, rising from his seat. "My steward is preparing your first installment now, so you may take it with you. Will you promise to write to me on occasion, and let me know how you and Artie fare?"

"I promise."

He took her hand and bowed over it, as if she were still a proper lady. "Then I will bid you farewell, Miss Lockwood."

She offered him a rather unpracticed curtsy and bid him farewell in return, practically running up the staircase to Mrs. D. and Miss H. in their chamber.

"At least one thing has gone right," she told them, as Mrs. D. opened the door and waved her inside. "I have been acknowledged by my cousin as part of the family, and he has settled an allowance on me large enough to meet my needs."

Mrs. D. sighed heavily and put her arms about Olivia. "Thank heavens for that!"

"Wonderful," Miss Hatch said, releasing a sigh of her own from her place on the settee by the window. "That will be a weight off your shoulders."

"And yours," Olivia smiled, glancing from one pair of shining eyes to the other. "The two of you will no longer need to worry about me making ends meet."

"You will still join us for dinner some nights, won't you?" Mrs. D. asked, releasing her hold on Olivia.

Miss H. added, "That is, if you're going to return with us to Wales."

A weighty weariness settled over Olivia like a wet blanket. "I want nothing more than to sleep in my own bed again."

"Then you'd better speak to His Grace," Mrs. D. said with a frown.

"Do you still think he's evil?" Olivia teased.

But Mrs. D. didn't take the bait. "He has helped you, and for that I will always be grateful. But yes, I still think he is a bad man."

He'd confessed to being such when he'd proposed, wanting her to know who she would be shackling herself to if she accepted. She thought he might have been exaggerating slightly, playing to his dark reputation in an effort to balance out the wealth and power he offered her.

Olivia shook her head. "After we return home again, I suppose it matters not if he's an immoral brute. He will go back to being the distant landlord he was before."

Miss H. was nodding, but Mrs. D. looked unconvinced.

"Then you should go tell him you want to return with us," Mrs. D. finally said. "And we'll be home that much faster."

Olivia allowed herself to be turned and walked out the door with a laugh, then set about finding Rhuddlan and making arrangements to travel back to Wales. She found him, not in his chamber where she expected him to be, but in the coach-house inside their borrowed—or perhaps traded—carriage.

"What are you doing in there?" she asked with a laugh. He was down on all fours on the floor of the carriage, one booted foot hanging out the door.

"Olivia?" He got to his feet and climbed out, his black hair slightly mussed. "Did you conclude your business with Teverton?"

"Yes."

"Judging by the smile on your face, the outcome was satisfactory," he said, offering her a little smile of his own.

"It was. And I thank you for bringing me here." She stepped closer to him, reaching tentatively for his hand. "You and his lordship have given me my life back."

He clasped her hand and brought it to his chest. "That's what I was hoping for. Does that mean you'll be returning to Wales with me?"

She followed her hand closer to Rhuddlan. "Yes. I'm ready to go home."

"Excellent." He kissed her hand, and led her to the open carriage door. "I want to show you something before we depart. Don't tell Mrs. Davies and Miss Hatch—I think it would unsettle them to know there's a weapon beneath their feet."

"What?"

He leaned in and slid his fingers inside a slit in the carpet. "There's a small dagger hidden here. It's just a precaution. I very much doubt you'll need it, but I feel more comfortable knowing it's here."

"You think Sir George...?"

Rhuddlan shook his head. "You are free of him. I promise you that."

Mrs. D.'s words impugning his character came back to her and she frowned. "What did you do to him?"

"Do you really want to know?" he asked, his brows raised.

She didn't really *want* to know, but she needed to. "Yes."

"I beat him senseless," Rhuddlan said slowly. "And that's not a figure of speech. He was bloody and broken and terrified, and I left him there in that meadow."

"Could he have died there?" The words nearly wouldn't come, but she had to know.

"Teverton sent men to look for him, but he was nowhere to be found."

She released a breath she'd unconsciously held and nodded, not knowing what else to say. Rhuddlan had nearly beaten a man to death...for her.

And now he was showing her the dagger he'd hidden in the carriage.

"If he lives he may come for me again," she said, trying to keep her voice steady.

Rhuddlan shook his head. "Grayson is a gambler, and a bad one. I sent instructions to Lewis to buy up Grayson's outstanding debts from whomever holds them. By the time we return to Wales, I will be his sole creditor. If he recovers from the beating I gave him, I'll call in his debts and reduce him to utter poverty."

She turned their clasped hands over and studied his —the knuckles red and swollen, a scar across the back. What did she do now with the information he'd given her?

She nodded, more to herself than to Rhuddlan, and met his eyes. "Thank you for telling me." She took another breath, then blew it out. "So if the dagger isn't for protection against Sir George, it's for protection against your brother."

"I don't think he'll harm you," Rhuddlan said, squeezing her hand. "It's me he wants. But I thought it prudent to be prepared, just in case." He released her hand and pulled the gold signet ring from his finger, holding it up for her to see. "I'm putting this in there, as well. If something happens to me, take this ring back to Rhuddlan Hall and let Lewis know."

She watched as he slid the ring under the carriage carpet beside the dagger, nodding once again without words. The very last thing she ever wanted to do was return to Rhuddlan Hall without its master.

They parted then, Rhuddlan wanting to check on the horses while Olivia returned to the house to pack her things. A few hours later, they were seated side by side in the carriage studiously not looking at each other for more than a few moments at a time. Mrs. D. and Miss H. exchanged a few glances of their own, and Olivia knew they were trying to figure out what was different. But whatever Olivia felt for Rhuddlan was something she had to discern for herself.

She laid her head back against the squabs and closed her eyes, ignoring the brass buttons in her lap that she was supposed to be sewing to a tailcoat for a customer, trying to clear her mind of everything but the sway of the carriage and the clip-clop of the horses' shoes on the road. It worked for a time, until the carriage came to a halt.

"Stand and deliver, Luca!"

Olivia sat up and looked at Rhuddlan. "Luca?"

He nodded, his lips pressed in a firm line. "Stay here."

Chapter Eight

RHUDDLAN CLIMBED OUT of the carriage, shutting the door firmly behind him. Perhaps if he gave himself up, Nick would allow the women to continue on unharmed.

"Here I am, Nicu." Rhuddlan raised his arms over his head. "And I'm unarmed."

Three men with pistols stood in a triangle around the carriage—two at the back and one near the front—pointing their weapons at him, but none of the men was Nick.

Rhuddlan's brother came into view around the front of the carriage, carrying their grandfather's ornate flintlock pistol loosely in his hand. "We meet again at last."

"We could have met plenty of times before this, Nicu, without involving weapons and innocent people."

"You had a chance to stop this before it ever got this far," Nick said, putting his free hand over his heart with false innocence. "You could have stopped it all at any time."

"Don't make this out to be my fault," Rhuddlan countered. "It was you and your men running around setting fires, committing assault, destroying people's lives."

Nick smiled broadly. "I believe I learned that last one from my big brother." Rhuddlan scoffed, but Nick continued, "Isn't that what you did to George Grayson?"

No one but Teverton and Olivia knew about Rhuddlan's set-to with Grayson, and only Olivia and Lewis knew about the plan to ruin him financially. How did Nick find out about any of it? "He was getting violent with some of my tenants. All I did was warn him off."

"With your fists." Nick walked slowly up to Rhuddlan and punched him in the stomach without warning. "Like that?"

Rhuddlan doubled over, tears streaming down his face as he gasped for air. His knees buckled and he folded onto the road, his forehead crashing into a rock that was embedded in the dirt. Before he could get his breath back or check his head for blood, hands grabbed both his arms and hoisted him to his feet.

"Or maybe like this."

Another blow delivered, this time to his face. Fortunately, Nick's boxing days were long past and the punch didn't break any bones. But it hurt like the devil and Rhuddlan sucked in a breath.

He was momentarily distracted by a scuffle approaching the carriage door, and the barking of a dog. Rhuddlan forced his eyes to focus, watching two of Nick's men dragging John Coachman between them and force him into the carriage.

"If you hurt him..." But kneeling on the road with blood coursing down his face, Rhuddlan knew he wasn't much of a threat.

"Load him up," Nick ordered, flashing his brother a smile, and the two men restraining Rhuddlan hauled him to a second carriage that was turned ninety degrees from the direction of travel, blocking the road. Nick followed behind and hopped into the carriage after his men had thrown Rhuddlan onto the floor.

"Take whatever valuables they have in the carriage," Nick told them. "Do what you want with the occupants."

"Leave them alone," Rhuddlan commanded hoarsely. "Those women have done nothing to you."

Nick leaned down, grinning. "But they're something to you, aren't they?"

Rhuddlan's feet were shoved inside the carriage and the door was slammed shut. A moment later they were in motion and Rhuddlan scrambled on to the seat, praying Nick was only toying with him, that Olivia and her neighbors would be left alone.

Rhuddlan reached for the curtain covering the carriage window, but Nick raised the barrel of the pistol.

"No you don't. You'll see where we're going when we get there."

They rode along in silence after that, Nick with that stupid grin on his face and Rhuddlan with his arms crossed over his chest. He wasn't sure how much time had passed—Nick wouldn't allow him to check his pocket watch, either—but the carriage finally came to a halt and the door was once again opened.

"Out," Nick commanded.

Rhuddlan, lacking a better option, obeyed, and was hustled into a squat cabin surrounded by dense woods. His guards forced him down onto a rough chair and tied his arms and legs to it, then disappeared from the room.

"Are you going to say something trite like, 'I've got you now'?" Rhuddlan asked in a conversational tone. "Or are we going to skip right to the ransom demand?"

"You've got it all wrong, brother dear," Nick said, coming to stand before Rhuddlan. "There won't be any ransom. You can either turn over control of the dukedom to me voluntarily, or I'll take it from you as your heir."

Rhuddlan hoped he didn't visibly react to that statement. He'd always known it was Nick's goal, but hearing your own brother say directly to you that he wanted you dead was still a blow.

"You'll never have the title as long as I'm alive," Rhuddlan reminded him. "No matter what you control."

"True," Nick conceded. "I suppose that's another reason to kill you, then."

"You sound like the villain in a gothic novel," Rhuddlan said, shaking his head.

Nick laughed. "You would know."

Rhuddlan supposed that was a slur against his reading habits, but he had bigger things to worry about. Like the butt of his grandfather's pistol that was fast approaching his face.

The blow landed with a crunch that told Rhuddlan his nose had broken this time, if the pain hadn't already relayed that message. He let out a yell as warm blood began to ooze down his face, then fought a rising tide of panic when he realized he could no longer breathe properly.

Breathe through your mouth, Lucas, you idiot. It was the voice of his older brother when they were adolescents, when Hadley had accidentally dunked him in the pond one summer. Rhuddlan's nose had filled with water that took a minute to find its way out once he'd been pulled onto the bank.

Hadley's voice calmed him enough to take stock of his condition, and to begin breathing though his mouth.

Nick didn't react at all.

"I'm not going to give over all those people's lives to you, Nick," he said, spitting blood onto the planked floor. He focused on the face of his baby brother, still only five-and-twenty with his whole life ahead of him.

"Why not? Perhaps I'd be a better duke than you," he said matter-of-factly. "It's a shame birth order determines who controls such a vast empire, or I might not have had to resort to this."

The next blow came not from Nick's fist, but from a sharp object being plunged into Rhuddlan's thigh. He threw back his head, but clenched his teeth against the scream trying to tear from his throat. He dearly didn't want to give his tormentor the satisfaction of watching him writhe in pain.

"Those sound like Cumberland's words," Rhuddlan muttered when he could trust his voice again. Cumberland had, in fact, expressed a similar opinion when his new niece, who preceded him in the succession to the throne, was born earlier this year. Would Cumberland resort to plotting the little princess's death to become King of England? Probably not.

But Nick was willing to kill to become the Duke of Rhuddlan.

"Oh, he might have mentioned it once or twice. It was my idea to do something about it," Nick said, disappearing through an interior doorway for a moment. He returned with an old, battered fowling piece. "You're about to have a hunting accident."

Rhuddlan must have given Nick an incredulous look, because Nick continued, "It can't look like *I* did it, or I'll hang for murder."

"Why are you doing this, Nicu?" Rhuddlan asked weakly. The physical punishment had been bad enough, but looking into the face of his own brother every time it was delivered had taken a greater toll on him. "What did I ever do to you to deserve this?"

"What did you do?" The question seemed to freeze Nick in his tracks. "Nothing, Lucas. When Mama died, you did nothing. When Hadley died, then Father, you did *nothing* for me. I was left in the care of nurses and tutors while my closest living relative spent his days elsewhere." His eyes shifted to a space behind Rhuddlan, then re-focused. "If Cumberland hadn't taken an interest in me, I'd probably still be buried under my books wondering where you were."

Tears came to Rhuddlan's eyes again, and this time he couldn't hold them back. "Oh, Nicu, I'm so sorry. I was only sixteen when Mama died, and didn't know what to do with my own grief."

"I was seven!" Nick bellowed, gesturing with the fowling piece.

"I know. I should have done better for you, especially after Father. I was just—"

"Just too busy being Rhuddlan to pay your little brother any heed," Nick finished, his face turning red with anger. "You were the one person in my life that I was supposed to be able to trust, and you chose the dukedom over me." He took aim with the fowling piece. "Now you'll have neither. And you won't have to worry about your duchess-to-be, either. If she's carrying your heir, she won't be for long."

Rhuddlan strained at the ropes that bound him to the chair. "What have you done to Olivia?"

The next thing he knew, Nick was face down on the floor and the fowling piece was skittering across the room.

"He did nothing to me," his rescuer said through gritted teeth, digging her knee into Nicks back and pressing the barrel of a pistol to his head. "Do you feel that? Move and I'll pull the trigger."

"You had a chance to stop this before it ever got this far."

Olivia huddled with Mrs. D. and Miss H. in the carriage, trying to quell the trembling that seemed to have pervaded every one of her limbs. This was what Rhuddlan had feared—his brother finally catching up with them.

It was like being cornered by Sir George all over again.

"With your fists."

The subsequent groans had her peeking out the window, stifling a cry when she saw Rhuddlan in a heap on the road. Artie was barking, ears laid back, hackles up, as if to let the men outside know the carriage was off limits. Olivia tried to quiet him—the last thing they needed was more attention from the men with guns.

The door opened then and John Coachman was shoved inside, bleeding from his temple. He was alive, though, and still mostly of sound mind. "I'm sorry I couldn't hold 'em off, ladies. I did the best that I could, but when a man has a gun pointed at you, you don't argue."

"You did the right thing," Olivia assured him. "If you had resisted or angered those men, they might well have killed you."

"They're taking His Grace away!" Mrs. D. interrupted, pointing at the carriage blocking their path.

"Someone needs to be in that carriage," Miss Hatch said, "and leave a trail so we can find it again. The rest of us will have to overpower the men Lord Nicholas left behind and go for help."

Olivia straightened, glancing at the handful of brass buttons in her lap. She hadn't started sewing them onto their intended coat yet, and they were large and shiny.

"I'll do it," she said quickly, holding up one of the buttons. "These should make good markers."

Mrs. D. and Miss H. made a bit of a fuss, but Olivia swiftly subdued it with a raised hand. "We don't have time to argue. Let me do this."

The two older women exchanged a look, and Mrs. D. nodded. "Go quickly, then. And don't let them see you."

Olivia hurriedly dumped the buttons back inside the pouch they'd come in and glanced out the carriage windows. One of the men was dragging Rhuddlan to the other carriage, while the other two were watching.

"Can you distract them?" she asked, gesturing to the two behind the carriage.

"Oh, yes ma'am," John Coachman said, perking up. "You just be careful."

"You, too," she said, squeezing his shoulder. "All of you. Artie," she whispered into the dog's ear, despite his continued barking, "take care of them for me."

John changed places with Olivia, then opened the door on the right-hand side of the carriage, moaning loudly. As she'd hoped, both of Lord Nicholas's men rushed to him, and she slipped out the other door. She paused for the tiniest fraction of a second then took off running as fast as she could, clutching the pouch of buttons in one hand.

Lord Nicholas's carriage was already in motion by the time she reached it, and there was no time to secret herself on it. She jumped onto the back, grasping the handle meant for a footman who would often be stationed there during travel, then held her breath. The curtains were closed over all the windows, and the coachman did not seem to notice an extra passenger. Had she escaped detection?

When she was convinced she'd been unseen, she shifted her body into a more secure position, stowing the pouch of buttons inside the neckline of her dress and holding on to the handle with both hands. Every so often, she would reach into the pouch and toss out a button, fervently praying they wouldn't be disturbed before her friends could return with help.

If they had managed to overpower the two men Lord Nicholas had left behind.

Her hands and arms ached with a force she hadn't felt since the first time she'd gathered her own firewood. She'd only had a small hatchet borrowed from a neighbor, and she'd only managed to take down a couple of half-dead saplings, but the effort had required the use of muscles that had never been asked to do more than run a needle through fabric.

I managed that. I can manage this, too.

By the time the carriage came to a halt, Olivia's arms were dead weight. She had just enough strength left to get herself off the carriage and crouch down as Rhuddlan and his brother got out. She heard scuffling, but didn't dare try to get a look. Once the sounds had faded, though, she peeked around the corner. They had driven to a small, squat shelter in a wooded area and the footprints in the dirt indicated multiple people had gone inside.

Just as she was about to make a break across the open drive to the exterior wall of the structure, two men came out of the front door. One was dressed like a coachman, and made for the horses. The other was dressed like a laborer and walked a little way into the woods. When the carriage started to move Olivia had to make a quick decision, and dashed behind a large tree trunk. The coachman led the horses around the structure and began to unhitch them, while the other man... Apparently he needed to take care of some personal business.

And he'd left his pistol on a stump a couple of feet away.

Wishing desperately for breeches or trousers, she made her way toward the laborer as quietly, yet swiftly, as she could. He stood with his back to her, humming to himself, and she ran the last few feet without breathing. A twig snapped under her foot and he turned, his eyes wide when he saw who had made the noise. As he frantically tried to stuff himself in and button the falls of his trousers, she darted the last few feet and snatched the pistol from the stump, training it on the main with her exhausted arms.

He raised his hands halfway into the air, but his tone was smug. "You're not going to shoot me."

No, Olivia likely wouldn't shoot unless he came at her. But she had something much better than that in her bag of tricks. "What is your employer going to say when he finds out a woman took your pistol from you? That you were caught unawares during an important job by a seamstress?"

The man paled visibly. He could try to take the pistol away from her, but the instant he moved toward her he risked being shot. He could call for help from the coachman, but then there would be a witness to his folly. And if Lord Nicholas was the kind of man who would beat and kidnap his own brother, she could only imagine what he would do to an employee who'd been bested by a scared female.

"Keep it," the man finally said. "Just let me have a head start before you go in there."

She nodded and he took off through the woods, leaving Olivia dangling her arms and silently, slightly hysterically, laughing.

Then she gathered herself—Rhuddlan was injured and at the mercy of his fratricidal brother, and there was still a coachman somewhere on the property who could give her presence away at any moment.

Olivia hid herself behind a tree once more and took stock of her situation. The coachman was nowhere in sight, nor were her friends. She was exhausted, in pain, carrying a loaded pistol, and all on her own. Tears welled in her eyes at the hopelessness of it all and she sank down to the ground.

"What can I even do?"

A man's bellowing voice rang out from inside the shelter and she instinctively jumped to her feet, reassessing. "I'm all he has right now..."

She took a deep breath and ran to the little building, pausing just long enough to hear two voices, then flung open the door. There before her stood Lord Nicholas aiming a long barreled gun at Rhuddlan.

"What have you done to her?" Rhuddlan was yelling.

Olivia was in motion before she'd consciously made the decision to run, launching herself at Lord Nicholas and knocking him to the ground.

"He did nothing to me." She recovered her awareness before Lord Nicholas and scrambled to pin him down, kneeing him in the back. Then she realized she was still holding the laborer's pistol, and she pressed the tip of the barrel to the back of his head. "Do you feel that? Move and I'll pull the trigger."

She was shaking and sweaty and terrified, but the gun Lord Nicholas had been holding was several feet away and he was not struggling beneath her.

And Rhuddlan—

Rhuddlan was alive.

She bowed her head and squeezed her eyes shut, her face hidden by a curtain of hair that had come loose during her mad dash. Rhuddlan was tied to a chair and looked as though he'd been beaten, but he was breathing and blinking and speaking.

"Olivia?"

She lifted her head and pushed her hair from her face. "Yes, Your Grace?"

He laughed a little at that, and a great wave of relief swept through her body.

"Are you hurt?" he asked.

He was tied to a chair with blood on his face and clothes, but he was inquiring about her welfare? She started giggling. "I may sleep for a few days when we are finally safe again, but for now I'll do. You, I suspect, could do with the services of a physician."

He nodded slowly. "I daresay you're right. You don't, by any chance, have one on the way do you?"

"No, but I'm hoping reinforcements will be arriving soon."

Lord Nicholas squirmed under her weight, and she pulled his ear as if he were a naughty little boy. "Be still, my lord. I do still have a pistol to your head."

Of all the words she'd said in her thirty years on earth, those were thirteen she'd never expected to utter. But they worked, and Lord Nicholas became still again.

"Do you hear that?" she asked not a moment later.

"What?" Rhuddlan countered in a thick voice.

Olivia smiled. "Barking. I hear Artie barking."

His whole body relaxed and his lips curved into a weak smile. "Good."

Lord Nicholas stirred suddenly then, rising up beneath her and unceremoniously dumping her to the floor. Olivia landed on her right arm, trapping the pistol under her body until she could get her bearings again and roll over. By that point, though, her arm had been asked to do too much and it refused to lift the pistol and prepare to fire it.

Fortunately, Olivia's body was between Lord Nicholas and the long gun. He glanced at it for a moment, but must have thought better than to make an attempt at it. Instead, he shot an unreadable look at his brother and disappeared out the door.

Chapter Nine

A FEW HOURS later, they were all safely ensconced in a tiny inn with roaring fires and the innkeeper's wife's freshly baked bread and new cheese. The innkeeper had also obligingly fetched a physician, who was finishing up with his last patient: Artie, at Rhuddlan's specific request. He'd been grazed by a bullet during the escape from Nick's men and was bleeding a little. The physician had balked at treating a dog, but Rhuddlan had insisted. Artie had bitten one of the gun-toting men so hard he'd broken the man's hand, helping to ensure the immediate safety of three people, and the later rescue of his mistress and Rhuddlan himself. Artie deserved the best care available in return for his bravery, and the physician's conclusion—that the dog should recover quickly—set Olivia's mind at ease.

Olivia herself had been seen to and had received the same pronouncement, suffering cuts and scrapes and crushing fatigue, but nothing worse, setting Rhuddlan's mind more at ease. His own situation was a little more serious, but he allowed himself to be put to bed per the physician's orders after his leg would had been dressed and his nose set. He carefully ate some of the bread and cheese, then collapsed back onto his pillows.

Before he could drift off to the sleep his body was clamoring for, a knock sounded on his door. "It's Olivia."

"Enter," he called, struggling to sit up. Not only was his body weary from his ordeal that afternoon, but the physician had given him a dose of laudanum to ease the pain of his injuries.

"The messengers you asked for have arrived, Your Grace."

His heart fell slightly at the formality of her words, but he pushed past the feeling. There was business to attend to. "Good. The messages are there," he said, pointing to three sealed letters on the only table in the room. There was one for Teverton, a warning in case Nick learned the viscount had harbored Rhuddlan and wanted retribution. The note to Lewis requested a full complement of guards and outriders be sent to escort Rhuddlan and his party home. And one for Sussex requesting his presence at Rhuddlan Hall at his earliest convenience. "There are coins for each of them—"

"I see them," she confirmed, reaching for the letters and their accompanying pouches. "I'll take these down and get them on their way."

He shook his head reprovingly. "You should be resting, Miss Stone." Would he ever learn to call her Miss Lockwood? Did it matter to her?

She didn't indicate one feeling or another about her name. She only smiled at his concern. "This is the last thing I'll do, then I will lie down."

"Will you come back and lie down with me?" He asked, raising his eyebrows hopefully.

"Artie will come and sit with you for a while," she replied in a neutral tone. "Perhaps we'll all get the rest we need."

She was gone for a few minutes, then returned as promised with her dog. Artie's head was bandaged and he was moving more slowly than usual, but he otherwise looked all right. He went right to the fireplace and settled himself on the rug there, his eyes closing for a well-deserved nap.

"He's made himself right at home," Olivia chuckled.

"Good," Rhuddlan replied. "You should, too."

She came to sit on the edge of his bed, smoothing a hand over his battered face. "You should stop worrying about me for a while and rest."

"Let me do one last thing for you, then I'll rest," he said, allowing his eyes to close briefly at her touch.

"What's that?"

"I want to void our agreement regarding your cottage," he said softly. Her blue eyes went wide, the fear in them easily discernible, and he reached for her hand. "I want to give you a small piece of property, instead. It's several miles from the village, but it has a snug little house and a sturdy stable. You could have a large kitchen garden if you wanted one, or keep small livestock—"

Her mouth had gone round at his pronouncement, but she chuckled at that. "For Artie to herd?"

"A fellow has to feel useful," he replied with a grin. Then he became serious. "You saved my life, Olivia. If not for you and Mrs. Davies and Miss Hatch, Nick would have killed me today."

Tears welled up in her eyes, and she swiped them away. "Don't forget Artie and John Coachman," she said.

"Never," he smiled. "I am going to offer John an early pension for his efforts, and Mrs. Davies and Miss Hatch will have their home for as long as they require it. But you," he ran his thumb over the back of her hand, "you put yourself in harms way to save me."

The idea of proposing marriage again entered his mind, but he elected not to do it despite the longing for her that had been building since his kidnapping. All the logical reasons he'd presented her with were still valid —he needed an heir, they got along well together, and a woman alone in the world could always use protection. But he could merely be experiencing immense gratitude and mistaking it for affection, or a heightened sense of protectiveness for the woman who'd put herself in danger for him. In any case, she'd already turned him down once and had given no indication that she'd welcome a second offer.

She squeezed his hand and brushed away another tear with her free hand. "I suppose that makes us even, then."

"Not quite," he smiled. "Will you let me see you and Artie settled?"

"But I cannot reward you for your bravery in saving me," she protested.

"The only reward I need is knowing you're safe and well." It sounded trite even as Rhuddlan said the words aloud, but it was the truth, and he didn't know how better to express the sentiment.

She didn't reply for a long moment, but then nodded. "Then yes. And we'll both thank you for it."

"It is truly my pleasure," he murmured, bringing her hand to his lips for a kiss.

She followed her hand down and pressed her lips to his in a gesture he hadn't expected, but welcomed. He released her hand and slid his arms around her, smiling against her mouth when she reciprocated.

"Does this mean I'm not 'Your Grace' any longer?" he asked, dropping a kiss on the corner of her mouth.

"I wasn't sure..." Her voice trailed off, then she started again. "I wasn't sure what our relationship was anymore. After the things we've told each other, the things we've done..."

"Wonder no longer," he said softly, finally finding the strength to sit up. He slid a hand into her hair and kissed her deeply, his heart racing when she tightened her arms around him and kissed him back. He broke off much sooner than he would have liked in deference to his swollen nose, but trailed several kisses along her cheek.

"I care very much for you, Olivia," he murmured in her ear, sliding one hand over the fabric of her gown to cup her breast. "If my body was in better condition, I'd show you just how much."

She moaned softly and Rhuddlan was nearly ready to defy the physician's orders, laudanum or no. He was hard and ready, but he had no strength or stamina left and sighed instead, defeated.

"Another time," she whispered, grinning.

"Don't tease me, sweetheart," he laughed. Her whole demeanor flipped on its head in an instant and he arched an eyebrow. "Grayson?"

She nodded, dropping her forehead to his shoulder.

"He deserves to rot in hell for what he's done to you," Rhuddlan said, clenching his jaw. Then he had a marvelous idea. "I promise you, Olivia Lockwood Stone, that I will give you all the pleasure you could ever want when I'm able once again."

She drew back and met his gaze. "You will?"

"If you want me to," he said seriously. "You deserve to know all the ways you like to be touched and tasted, to lie with a man who will worship your body, and to put George Grayson and his loathsome conduct out of your mind forever."

"You want to worship my body?" she asked as red crept up her neck and into the cheek he had been kissing only moments ago.

"God yes," he said in a rough voice, kneading the breast he still held.

Her eyes closed and she moaned again. "But not tonight," she said, rather breathlessly.

"No," he replied, and he heard the profound disappointment in his own voice.

Olivia must have heard it too, for she grinned. "You will simply have to rest up and heal quickly, then," she said in a low voice. "I'm going to want you at your best."

She rose from her place on the bed, covering his hand on her breast with her own and clasping his fingers. "Sleep well, Mr. Blake."

She crossed the room and opened the door slowly, glancing at Artie, fast asleep before the fire. "Do you mind if he stays here for a while? I don't want to wake him."

Rhuddlan looked over at the dog, curled into a ball on the only rug in the room. "Let him sleep," he decided. "Perhaps we'll recuperate better together."

Olivia smiled gently and blew them each a kiss before closing the door behind her. Rhuddlan sighed, envious of Artie's deep sleep but fading into fatigue himself.

"It's better that she left," he muttered to himself, dropping back down onto his bed and trying to make his battered body comfortable. "That one night of pleasure I promised her might be all we have together. I want to make it wonderful for her, and not have to worry about suffocating when we kiss because my nose hasn't healed properly."

He wouldn't say it aloud or even admit it to himself, but he also wanted to make memories he could look back on after they'd parted. If one night was all he was going to get with her, he would damn well make it the best night either of them had ever had.

They remained at the inn until the guard Rhuddlan had sent for arrived from Rhuddlan Hall, then proceeded at a leisurely pace back to Wales in deference to the injured, including himself. He spent the greater part of the journey asleep or nearly so, thanks mostly to the laudanum and the trauma his body had endured. When he was awake and alert, Olivia was by his side reading to him, playing cards with him, or just talking as she sewed.

They had no further word from Nick, but Rhuddlan knew his brother wasn't going to simply fade away into the countryside. As the carriage neared home, he waved off his next dose of laudanum to confront the issue.

"Nick is still out there," he said, meeting the eyes of the three women in the carriage with him, "and he knows who you are—especially you, Miss Stone." He brushed the side of his hand discreetly against hers, suppressing a shudder as he remembered the sick feeling that had begun to consume him when Nick had threatened Rhuddlan's "duchess-to-be."

"What do you suggest, Your Grace?" Miss Hatch asked, paling.

"That you return with me to Rhuddlan Hall until I can apprehend my brother," he answered. "I'm afraid it will be a bit like being under house arrest, likely for all of us."

"As it was before we went to Teverton Estate," Mrs. Davies said with a nod. "I miss my garden, Your Grace, but there are worse places to be confined."

Olivia grinned. "You enjoyed your time at Rhuddlan Hall, did you?"

"Yes," Mrs. Davies said sheepishly. Then she became more serious, adding, "And I would rather be safely tucked away than take the chance of repeating any part of this week."

"Well said," Olivia replied soberly.

"Miss Hatch?" Rhuddlan asked the silent member of the group.

She nodded. "They're right. I miss my home, too, but if we are safer at Rhuddlan Hall, then we will accept your invitation, Your Grace."

"Good," he said, hoping his excitement didn't show overmuch. He was pleased to be keeping the promise he'd made Olivia regarding her safety, of course. He was also very much looking forward to having her with him on a daily basis. Perhaps they would be able to spend some time together that didn't involve being hunted.

His daydreams of domestic bliss were temporarily abandoned when they arrived at Rhuddlan Hall. Footmen rushed to the carriage to help the disembarking passengers and bring in their luggage, as usual, but this time Lewis was among them.

"Welcome home Your Grace. How are you feeling?" he asked.

"I'll live," Rhuddlan replied. "How is Vaughn faring?"

"He wants to return to work," Lewis smiled. "But the physician says not yet."

Rhuddlan allowed himself a small smile. "That's a good sign."

"The Duke of Sussex is here, as well, Your Grace," Lewis continued. "He arrived yesterday."

"That is not a good sign," Rhuddlan sighed. "I asked him to come, but I didn't expect he'd be here so soon. Where is he now?"

"Reading in the library, Your Grace."

"I'll see him in my study directly."

Lewis bowed and returned to the house, and Rhuddlan turned to his guests. The housekeeper was already leading Mrs. Davies and Miss Hatch toward the front door, but Olivia had lagged behind a few steps with Artie. Rhuddlan caught up to her laid a hand on her shoulder.

"Miss Stone?"

She turned, smiling when she met his eyes. "Yes, Your Grace?"

The dog nudged his hand, asking for a pat, and Rhuddlan obliged him. "Will you join me for cards after dinner?"

"I would be delighted."

He took her hand dropped a kiss on the back. "Then I will see you this evening."

She gave him one more smile, then called to Artie and went inside. Rhuddlan watched her for a moment, letting the thought of their evening together warm him in the cool autumn air. But only for a moment—Sussex was waiting.

"You look like hell," the prince said when Rhuddlan walked into his study, shutting the door behind him.

But there was no offer to talk later. "Well, my brother did try to kill me."

Sussex frowned, rising from the sofa he'd occupied to hand Rhuddlan a stack of newspapers. "When that didn't work, he asked Cumberland to send in reinforcements."

Rhuddlan scanned the papers, noting stories in each that centered around himself. Some of them merely rehashed old rumors, focusing mainly on his late wife and missing cousin. But there were new accusations mixed in: that he'd burned down the mill on his own estate because the miller stole grain from him, that he had beaten Vaughn nearly to death for being disrespectful, that he had debauched a local seamstress and made her his mistress against her will. All quoting a "Duke of C." as one of their sources.

"Corruptions of the truth," Rhuddlan growled, flinging the papers onto his desk.

"Of course they are—that's how Cumberland plays this game," Sussex said. "Most people won't look below the surface of his claims. They'll see that the mill has indeed burned down, that Vaughn was certainly attacked, and that a young seamstress is in fact a guest in your home."

Rhuddlan ran his hands through his hair, tracing a finger over the scar on the back of his scalp. "And even if I can get the papers to print corrected stories, which is doubtful, no one will pay them any mind."

Sussex pressed his lips together and nodded.

"Wait, what is this?" Rhuddlan picked up one of the newspapers that had slid off his desk and fallen to the floor. "This one doesn't even pretend to be based on truth." He turned the paper face-out for Sussex to read, then turned it back for himself. "This one says I seduce women to drink their blood, and am immortal. How am I supposed to combat that nonsense?"

"You aren't," Sussex replied, resuming his seat on the sofa. "Or, at least, that's what Cumberland thinks. When Lord Nicholas failed to kill you physically, Cumberland began a campaign to kill you socially and politically."

"With stories like these, Nick can attempt to have me committed to an asylum and take control of the dukedom." Rhuddlan sighed heavily, and dropped into a nearby chair.

Sussex shook his head. "You are Rhuddlan until your death. Nick can't change that."

"I doubt it matters much to him whether or not people address him as Your Grace," Rhuddlan said, putting a hand to his head. "He would have plenty of money and power as my proxy, even if he was never granted the authority that comes with the title."

"Then you'd better be on your best behavior until you stop him," Sussex counseled. "Have you plans to wed anytime soon?"

He'd told no one of the offer he'd made Olivia, but he thought of her. In light of this new attack, it was good she'd refused him. But, just for a moment, he let himself imagine her as his wife. "No."

"You might want to start looking for someone who would make a suitable duchess. A sensible marriage to a lady of high birth would go a long way toward rehabilitating your reputation."

Rhuddlan didn't want a sensible marriage to a suitable lady, but he knew his friend was right. Anything that would raise his standing among the members of his class would weaken Nick's case for commitment when it was presented.

"I'll think about it," he replied without enthusiasm. "In the meantime, do you know any newspaper reporters who would like some interesting information about Cumberland?"

Rhuddlan and Sussex spent the rest of the afternoon together, trying to come up with a counter for Cumberland's new offensive. By the time they quit for the day, dinner had come and gone and Rhuddlan was exhausted.

Nevertheless, he was looking forward to the evening's entertainment and found himself smiling again when he entered the drawing room. Olivia was back to wearing her own clothing, worn and created without the least nod to what was fashionable, but she looked lovely sitting on his ornate sofa with a pool of cloth in her lap.

"Have you been waiting long?" he asked, shutting the door behind him and taking a seat beside her.

"We finished dinner an hour ago," she said with a small smile. "But I've had plenty to keep me busy."

"I'm sorry." He propped an arm up on the back of the sofa. "Sussex and I were trying to plan our next move, and time got away from me."

She put down the item she was sewing and reached her arm along the back of the sofa as well, touching her fingers to his. "Did you come up with something?"

"Possibly, but I'm not sure if it will work." He sighed heavily. "Sussex thinks I should take another wife. Someone of impeccable character and birth."

"Oh." There was a long pause before she spoke again, in a quieter voice. "Are you going to?"

He slid closer to her, taking her hand in his. "I'd rather not. At least, not for that reason. I will eventually need to wed again, for I need an heir that is not my brother. But I don't want Nick and Cumberland to dictate who it is I take to wife."

"Of course not."

He wanted to ask her if she'd considered marriage again, after the disaster that was her first fiancé. But he already knew the answer would be a resounding no—she'd been ruined socially and financially, then began living under an assumed name. The only time she'd likely considered matrimony was when George Grayson tried to blackmail her into it, and when Rhuddlan himself had proposed marriage.

Instead he sighed again. "Would you mind terribly if we didn't play cards tonight?"

The disappointment on her face was as clear as the newspapers he'd been reading, but she nodded. "I don't mind."

"I was hoping that we might just sit and talk...and hold each other."

Her eyes shifted from their clasped hands to his face. "Is that truly what you want to do?"

"Yes," he said, reaching for her. "I just want to relax and think about something happier than my brother's hatred for me."

She set her sewing aside and came into his arms, caressing his cheek, running a finger gently across his wounds. "That's fair. I don't particularly want to sit here with my thoughts, either."

"What were you thinking about?"

She laid her head on his shoulder. "How, if my mother hadn't been so selfish eight years ago, I wouldn't have been in a position for Sir George to terrorize me the way he did."

"You would have been a countess by now," Rhuddlan said, surprised by the fact as he said the words. "Windermere stuck his spoon in the wall a couple of years ago."

"A countess," she repeated softly, palming his chest. "How different that would have been."

He kissed her hair, aching for the life she'd been cheated out of. Perhaps she never loved Old Windy's heir, but he was a good fellow. And he'd have treated her a damn sight better than the life she ended up with.

"You and I would not be cuddling in your drawing room," she continued, planting a kiss on his lapel. "So at least one good thing has come of all the awfulness."

"But is this worth all the pain you've endured?" he asked. He probably knew the answer to his question, but he couldn't help asking it.

"Objectively? No. There's no way a few stolen moments of tenderness could compare to months of fear." She sat up, her blue eyes squarely meeting his gaze. "But being here in your arms I feel... I feel content. And I haven't had contentment in my life for too many years."

He bent his head and kissed her gently. "I'm glad I can give you that."

Rhuddlan wanted to give her so much more than mere contentment, but knew the likelihood of doing it was even lower now than it had been before, thanks to Nick and Cumberland's quest to prove him unfit.

He pushed the thought away, vowing to only think about the woman in his arms for the rest of the night.

Chapter Ten

A WEEK WENT by where every day had the same pattern: Olivia rose with the sun, worked on sewing for her customers, took breakfast with the rest of Rhuddlan's household, walked Artie, then brought out a special project she'd begun upon her return to Rhuddlan Hall. Evenings consisted mostly of dinner with Mrs. D. and Miss H. and an hour alone with Rhuddlan after he and the Duke of Sussex had finished for the day.

On the eighth morning, the pattern changed.

"Will you go for a drive with me this afternoon?" Rhuddlan asked over breakfast.

Olivia crunched a triangle of toast and nodded. "Where will we go?"

"It's a surprise," he said, the corners of his mouth turning up in a tiny smile. "I thought we'd take the curricle out, just the two of us."

They were the only two in the morning room at present—even the footmen serving had been dismissed —so Olivia let herself return his smile. "That sounds lovely."

And best of all, driving out together in an open vehicle like a curricle wouldn't be seen as inappropriate or compromising, if anyone was even around to see or care. She took another bite of her toast. Not that she worried for her own reputation anymore, but given the promises Rhuddlan had already made, he would likely insist on marrying her if he felt he'd compromised her. With her reputation in tatters and a horde of creditors itching to find her, she'd be the least appropriate woman to become a duchess since the Duke of Devonshire married his mistress. Rhuddlan already had enough trouble to deal with without piling more on him.

"Shall we say, two o'clock?" he asked, interrupting her thoughts.

"Yes," she answered. "That will give me time to finish taking in Mrs. Nesbitt's gown before we go, and I won't be worrying about it while we're out."

"Excellent. I want to have your undivided attention today."

They met in the stable at the appointed hour, where Rhuddlan was harnessing the horses himself. When he'd buckled the last buckle, he climbed up to the seat and offered her his hand. He was wearing gloves as a gentleman should, but Olivia hadn't had a pair of gloves for anything other than church since her mother's death, and she wished he had forgone his as well. Not because she felt inadequate—though she did— but because she'd become used to a degree of casual skin-to-skin contact with Rhuddlan and today they wouldn't have that. It was a small thing, but she found that she was rather disappointed by the prospect.

The drive was pretty, though, and Rhuddlan seemed happy to chat with her about inconsequential things—a relief after the both of them nearly being killed. He became quiet, though, as they turned onto a long drive.

"Have we arrived?" she asked.

"Mmhmm. See that little house there?" He pointed to a beautiful three-story house built of what looked like white limestone, with multiple chimneys bristling across the slate roof.

"It's beautiful," she sighed.

"It's yours."

Her eyes snapped away from the house and focused on the man beside her. "What?"

"This is the property I told you about, the one I want to give you in place of your cottage."

Her gaze swiveled back to the house, taking in the large windows that adorned the ground floor, the hedgerow that circled around toward the back of the dwelling, the large, manicured lawn that spread wide in all directions.

"Rhuddlan, it's too much. What would I do with so large a house?"

"Whatever you like," he said with a chuckle. "I wanted you to see it first, to be sure it would suit you. But I intend to sign the deed over to you with no restrictions, so you could live here, sell the place, turn it into a school..."

She linked her arm carefully with his while he brought the curricle to a halt. "You're very generous."

"You already agreed to let me see you settled properly, don't forget," he said with a smile. "Shall we take a look inside?"

He jumped down, securing the reigns to a low-hanging tree branch, then reaching up to help Olivia down. The curricle was taller than the carriages she was used to, and she had to put her hands on his shoulders while he held her by the waist. She landed practically in his arms, close enough to detect the lingering scent of his shaving soap.

They stood together for several moments, and for a fraction of a second Olivia thought he might kiss her. But he looked away, offering his arm instead and escorting her into the house.

"It has five bedrooms, plus a suite for the mistress of the house, a stillroom, a study, and all the usual reception rooms." He pointed out features he thought she'd like and explained the history of the furnishings as they toured the house. "Of course, if you'd like to redecorate, that is entirely your prerogative."

"Redecorate?" She had her allowance from Lord Teverton, and income from a few loyal customers. Perhaps she could purchase new items over time, but not if she or Artie became ill and needed to pay for a physician, or if her remaining customers took their custom elsewhere.

She didn't say that aloud, though. Rhuddlan's enthusiasm for the house and Olivia in it was bubbling over—she could see it in his sparkling green eyes, the smile that hovered on his lips—and she didn't want to dampen his mood.

"Or not," he replied, still smiling. "As you choose. Mr. and Mrs. Andersen can help you, as well."

"Mr. and Mrs. Andersen?"

"Servants," he clarified. "Mrs. Andersen cooks and cleans, and Mr. Andersen handles everything else.

"Oh."

He pulled her to a gentle halt in one of the bedchambers. "Part of the property is a small farm that has been leased to a local man," he said, taking her hand. "With the rent from the farm, you'll be able to pay the Andersens' wages, take care of any repairs the property might need, and still have a little left over."

The relief must have shown on her face because he took her other hand and gave it a squeeze. "I said I wanted to see you settled, didn't I? That meant making sure the property would make your life better, not burden you with more problems. I'm sure there is something I forgot or got wrong, but you need only tell me what and I'll take care of it."

She couldn't help but smile at that. His generosity was wonderful, of course, but she was particularly touched by his mindfulness of her situation. He could have easily given her a home that required an income well above what she actually possessed and not even noticed the strain it would place on her and her finances.

"Thank you, Rhuddlan. Artie and I both thank you very much."

They ended their tour in the study and Olivia was stuck by the difference between it and the rest of the house. The study walls were paneled in dark wood, carved with simple but elegant designs, a heavy mantle mounted over the fireplace, and what appeared to be a medieval shield with a stylized dragon at the center.

"Who lived here last?" she asked, running a finger along the edge of the desk set at one end of the room.

"My brother," he said softly. Her eyebrows shot up and he smiled, clarifying, "My older brother. He purchased this property as a sort of retreat, a place he could go when the world got to be too much. He could still ride into the village for a pint at the tavern if he wanted company, and there was plenty of room for guests. But this house is far enough away from almost everything else, so he could have peace and quiet when he needed it."

"That sounds wonderful," she breathed, taking his hand in hers.

He raised their clasped hands to his lips for a kiss. "That's why I thought of it for you. You can still take in work from village residents and your former neighbors, but if you prefer the solitude, that's available, too."

"You'll come to call sometimes, won't you?" she asked. "Artie will miss you when we're no longer lodging at Rhuddlan Hall."

"Artie will miss me?"

He arched a single eyebrow at her and she grinned. "He certainly will. And so will his mistress."

She released his hand and entwined her arms about his neck, gratified when he responded by wrapping his arms around her waist, flattening one warm hand against her back. They'd only known each other for a few weeks, but after all they'd been through together, after all the promises he'd made to her and kept, she felt safe with him.

She'd trusted him with her secrets, her very life, and he'd protected her with his own.

"We need not even contemplate separation for a time yet," he said, clearing his throat. "Not with Nick still at large. But yes, if you'd like me to call upon you once you take possession, I will."

"Good."

They strolled around the grounds for a time, then returned to the curricle for the return to Rhuddlan Hall.

"What do you think?" he asked, his eyes on the horses and the road before them.

"It's beautiful," she said, dropping a kiss on his shoulder.

"Can you picture yourself living there?"

It had been difficult when they'd first arrived—it had been years since she'd lived anywhere but her small cottage. But as they'd moved through the house she began to feel a bit like her old self, the daughter of a wealthy merchant who was used to directing servants and redecorating homes. It had been strange, and she wasn't entirely sure she wanted to return to the woman she'd been then. But perhaps she could forge a new life —the lady of the manor who could also fend for herself.

"Yes, I think I can."

"Wonderful," he grinned. "I'll have one of my secretaries draw up the papers right away."

A new home, an adequate income, a new life without Sir George. Once Lord Nicholas was dealt with, she would have everything she'd wanted and more.

So why didn't she feel as excited about it as Rhuddlan seemed to?

Rhuddlan spent the whole of the following day in his study putting his affairs in order. With his homicidal brother roaming free putting Rhuddlan's life in jeopardy, he wanted to make sure every single one of the thousands of people who depended upon him would be able to carry on without him.

And there was one person he especially wanted to protect.

He'd saved his will for last, knowing it would be the most complicated of the documents he'd need to modify. He looked at the list he'd made and began to write: a trust for Vaughn's care in the event he was still injured when Rhuddlan met his demise; monetary bequests to Mrs. Davies, Miss Hatch, John Coachman, and even Artie for distinguished service, as it were; annuities to his personal staff so they might choose whether or not to work for someone else; and the bulk of his unentailed property and the sum to properly manage and care for it all to Sussex, who didn't need the income but would see to the welfare of the tenants and employees involved. The entailed property would pass directly to his heir along with his titles, and that was still Nick unless Rhuddlan sired a son or Nick died before his brother.

But Rhuddlan Hall and the surrounding estate were not entailed, and he'd saved them specifically for one woman, whom he suspected he was in love with and had been for some time. He'd begun to think of her as "my Livie," though he knew they'd likely separate permanently, either when Nick was apprehended or when he finally succeeded in killing or incapacitating Rhuddlan. But she'd always have a place in his heart, and he was in a position to right at least one of the wrongs committed against her. He couldn't give her the title she'd been cheated out of, but he could make her as wealthy as a countess and answerable to no man.

He rose from his chair, stretching his body after too long in one position, and walked to the bell pull to summon a servant. Miss Stone's presence was requested when a footman arrived, and several minutes later she appeared in his doorway.

"You wanted to see me, Rhuddlan?"

She was wearing a new gown of white muslin with flowers printed in Rhuddlan red all over. She must have had one of the maids purchase it for her in the village upon their return from Liverpool—he'd heard Mrs. Davies and Miss Hatch urging her to make up something nice for herself once her work was completed, but she was still unsafe away from Rhuddlan Hall.

"Yes," he said, taking her hand and leading her over to his desk. "I want to show you something."

A knock sounded on the door before he could continue, followed by Lewis's voice. "Your Grace, two letters have come for you by messenger."

"Bring them in."

Lewis opened the door and delivered the letters to his master. "They came by different messengers, Your Grace."

"You've sent the messengers to the kitchen for something to eat?"

"Yes, Your Grace."

"Good."

"I'll leave you to your business," Olivia said, squeezing his hand before releasing it. "Whatever it is you want to show me can wait until this evening."

Lewis departed, but Rhuddlan reached for Olivia once more. "Wait a moment. These might concern you as well."

Rhuddlan broke the seal and scanned the first letter. It was a brief note from Sussex, who had returned to his own home near Shrewsbury, offering up two other possible solutions for Nick's confinement should he be captured. Sussex didn't come right out and say he thought Rhuddlan should do that rather than prosecute his brother for attempting to kill two people, along with all the other destruction he'd caused, but Sussex had already made his view on the subject clear. And transportation to a place where Nick couldn't hurt or manipulate anyone was an appealing idea—much more so than living with the knowledge that he was responsible for his own brother's execution.

He put Sussex's letter aside for the moment and opened the second letter. This one was from one of his ruffians, as George Grayson had called them, who had been out searching discreetly for Nick.

"They've found him."

"Found who?"

Rhuddlan looked up from the letter, frowning. "My people have found Nick."

"Wh-where is he?"

"Deganwy," he answered, mentally calculating how far away that was from Rhuddlan Hall. Around twenty miles as the crow flies; a day's ride on horseback in good weather.

Too close for comfort.

"He was trying to find passage aboard a boat bound for Ireland, but my people were able to detain him before he could depart."

She paled visibly. "Perhaps they should have let him go." When he raised a questioning eyebrow, she continued, "From Ireland he could have gone anywhere, disappeared into the world and never bothered us again."

Rhuddlan went to her, sliding his arms around her. "True. But now that he has been found and collected, I will know exactly where he is and who he is with at all times."

Her arms went around his shoulders and she held him tightly. "I think I prefer your way."

He sat down on the sofa with his arms still around her, settling her beside him. "So do I."

"What happens to him now?" she asked, laying her head on his shoulder.

"There are basically two choices," he began. A small voice in the back of his mind yelled that ladies were too delicate for such a conversation, but he silenced it. This lady was more than a match for what he was about to say. "I can have him arrested, then prosecuted for trying to kill me, among other things."

"Would it be a strong case?"

He nodded. "After he ambushed us on the way home from Teverton Estate, there was plenty of evidence to gather. No verdict can be guaranteed, of course, but he would likely be found guilty."

Olivia made a little gasping sound, and he tightened his arms around her.

"He'd hang," she said in a low voice. "What is the other choice?"

"That I discipline him myself, more or less," Rhuddlan answered. "Strip him of his money and privileges, and send him away to a remote corner of the world where I hope he won't do any more harm. If he were convicted by a jury, I could argue for his sentence to be commuted to transportation, but there's no guarantee the judge would agree."

"That's more humane."

"You're worried for his treatment?" Rhuddlan asked, drawing away so he could see her face.

She shook her head, grasping the lapel of his tailcoat between her thumb and forefinger. "More humane for you. How awful would it be for you if you had to advocate for your own brother's execution."

"Awful for my reputation or my conscience?" he asked, only partly in jest.

"Both, I imagine," she replied. "But I meant your conscience. If Lord Nicholas were convicted and hanged, you'd carry the guilt with you for the rest of your life. And if he were acquitted and released, you'd feel guilty over that as well, for he would be free to continue terrorizing you and the people who depend on you."

"It sounds like an easy solution, doesn't it? But what if he finds a way out of whatever hole I put him in and returns here?"

This was the heart of the matter for Rhuddlan. It seemed that, no matter which alternative he chose, he was bound to carry more guilt and anguish over it than the one who actually committed the crimes.

And there was only one scenario from which Nick could not return.

"I don't envy you this decision, that's for certain." She sighed and cuddled up against his chest once more. "What of the Duke of Cumberland? Have you any recourse against him?"

He kissed her hair, glad she was with him for this. "Very little. I know he's the one giving Nick ideas about how to conduct this campaign against me, and he's likely providing supplemental funding as well. But I can't prove it."

"So no prosecution of His Grace."

Rhuddlan shook his head and echoed her sigh. "No. The best Sussex and I have been able to manage is a few newspaper stories about Cumberland's misdeeds, based more in truth than those he had printed about me. I fear there won't be any further repercussions for him, and nothing to stop him from trying this a second time with someone else's disgruntled heir."

"That's nearly it, then, isn't it?" She smoothed an imaginary wrinkle from the front of his tailcoat. "Sir George, Lord Nicholas, the Duke of Cumberland... Our collective enemies have almost all been dealt with."

He started to smile, relieved to have his life coming back under his own control once more. But the end of their joint nightmare would also mean the end of their brief spell of domesticity. There would no longer be a reason for Olivia to remain at Rhuddlan Hall.

"There is one more thing," he said, remembering a final promise he'd made her and had yet to keep.

"What's that?"

"I promised to give you all the pleasure you could want once I'd healed." He ran his fingers down her arm, bare below the small cap sleeve of her gown, and she sucked in a breath.

"Yes, you did," she said slowly.

He couldn't tell how she felt about this last loose end of theirs, but his own heart was already starting to pound in anticipation and he knew she could feel it under her palm. "The decision is entirely yours, Olivia. If you'd rather not..."

She sat up and patted his nose gently, then touched a finger to the puncture wound on his thigh. "Have you healed sufficiently?"

The puncture wound was still somewhat tender, but his leg had held up to his regular activity rather well. And the swelling in his nose had gone down by the time he'd returned to Rhuddlan Hall after his kidnapping.

"I believe so," he said, trying to keep his voice even.

"That's good."

The corners of her mouth turned up slightly, and his breath quickened. "Does that mean you want to lie with me?"

"Yes," she nearly whispered.

"Tonight?"

Their night together could be a sort of celebration of their resilience in the face of danger, as well as a private goodbye. And it would give him something to think about other than what to do with his brother while he waited for Nick and his escort to arrive, which would be a pleasure in itself.

She nodded faintly at first, then with more conviction. "Tonight. Unless you plan to work later into the evening."

"Nothing could keep me from you, darling," he murmured. "Shall I come to you at ten o'clock?"

This time she shook her head. "Let me come to you. We'll have more privacy in your bedchamber."

Of course. Mrs. Davies and Miss Hatch were quartered in the same wing as Olivia, and he shuddered to think of what would happen if either woman heard what he hoped to be doing with their neighbor.

"As you wish."

Her breath caught, but she smiled. "I'd better let you return to your work, then."

She rose from the sofa, sliding her hand along his shoulders as she stood. He caught her fingers at the last moment and dropped a kiss on her knuckles.

"Until tonight."

He waited for her to close the door behind her, then he lolled his head back against the sofa and blew out a breath. After he'd collected himself, he rose and walked to his desk to dash off a note to Sussex. Rhuddlan still wasn't sure what punishment he could mete out for Nick, but one of Sussex's ideas had potential.

Olivia sat at the dressing table in her bedchamber later that night, wondering if she'd done the right thing in accepting Rhuddlan's invitation tonight. She certainly wanted the night of pleasure he'd promised her—there had been little enough of that in her life, particularly since her fiancé's departure. And she wanted pleasure with Rhuddlan. He was handsome, certainly, and she wouldn't deny her attraction to him. But more importantly he was considerate and thoughtful, and she knew she could trust him with something so intimate as her own body.

Yet, there was a little voice inside her head—one that sounded much like her mother—that continuously decried her decision. What about her virtue? Her reputation? Who would wed her if she gave herself to a man not her husband?

Olivia took the pins from her hair one by one, combing through her hair with her fingers as it came down and trying to silence the voice. Her virtue had already been given away, her reputation destroyed thanks to her own mother. No gentleman would wed her whether she went to Rhuddlan tonight or not.

She took up her brush and gently worked out the tangles in her hair. She wasn't so very worried about pregnancy, for she hadn't become pregnant by her fiancé. They weren't together enough times to conclude she was barren, certainly, but it was a possibility. And if she did get with child, she knew that Rhuddlan would care for both her and the babe.

"Then it's settled," she told the brush as she placed it back on the dressing table. "I am going to enjoy my time with him tonight without reservation, and with no regrets tomorrow."

She rose from the dressing table and briefly considered donning a nightdress, but decided against it. She had only two, and they were both rather plain, more so than even her daytime clothing. Walking into his bedchamber in such a flimsy, unlovely garment would make her feel self-conscious, and that was one emotion she refused to feel this night.

The clock on the mantle struck ten and she slipped from her chamber trying to appear nonchalant as she made her way to the master's suite. She passed a servant or two going about their tasks, but managed to hold her head up and conduct herself as if she were unashamed of what she was about to do. She *was* unashamed and the closer she drew to his door, the faster her heart beat.

Her knock was answered by Rhuddlan himself, who wore only his shirt, waistcoat, and trousers. He gestured her inside with a wide smile, and she tried not to stare at his bare feet—an intimate sight for an intimate evening.

"I'm glad you came."

"Did you think I wouldn't?"

"I wasn't sure, to tell you the truth," he said, shutting the door and locking it. "Society makes this a rather bigger undertaking for ladies than for gentlemen."

"Ah, but I am no longer a lady. I am simply Olivia Stone." She said it without bitterness or anger. For the first time since her mother's betrayal, she was glad not to be constrained by Polite Society's mandates for "proper" ladies. Tonight she was free to do as she pleased.

And it pleased her to bed the Duke of Rhuddlan.

"Well then, Olivia Stone, may I kiss you?"

She went into his arms and lifted her face to his, matching his smile when he slipped his arms around her, running a hand through her loose hair.

"It feels like silk," he murmured as he brought his mouth down over hers.

She laughed a little and broke the kiss. "It will be a mass of tangles tomorrow, so enjoy it while it lasts."

His bright eyes met hers and he nipped at her lips. "I intend to."

His mouth came down over hers, gently at first, then with more urgency. She tensed a little, anticipating the removal of her clothing, but it didn't happen. Rhuddlan drew back a fraction of an inch, breathing heavily already but with a question in his eyes.

She answered it with a smile, then captured his lips in a determined kiss. That seemed to be enough to satisfy his doubts, for he enthusiastically kissed her back, letting one hand slide across her body to cup her breast.

She moaned against his mouth and banished the little voice to the Outer Hebrides.

They spent several luscious moments kissing, learning the contours of each other's bodies. When one of his hands did begin working the buttons down the front of her gown, her blood was already on fire.

When enough buttons had been undone, he pushed her bodice from her shoulders and over her hips, sending her dress to the floor. Moments later her stays joined her dress and she stood there in nothing but her shift. His mouth found hers again and she could feel his heart racing beneath his shirt. She began working the buttons of his waistcoat, sliding it off his shoulders and down his arms.

"Olivia," he panted, breaking away. "When I'm inside you..."

She could feel herself blushing at his words, even as she pulled his shirt over his head and palmed his bare chest. "You won't be able to stop," she finished for him, trying not to frown at the idea. It was something her fiancé said to her once when they'd anticipated their vows in an old gamekeeper's cottage. He'd been gentle with her, and it had felt good, but he hadn't been wrong about his lack of stopping power.

He shook his head. "No. What I was going to say was that when I'm inside you, or at any point tonight, if you want me to stop all you have to do is let me know."

"Truly?"

"Truly," he said, meeting her eyes. Then he cupped her breasts, grinning when she moaned. "If this isn't pleasurable for both of us, there's no point."

"Then you'll have to tell me what is pleasurable for you, so I can be sure to do it." Her face was surely flaming now—talking about what they were about to do was very different than doing it.

He slid one strap of her shift down her shoulder and dropped several slow kisses down her neck. "We'll learn how to pleasure each other."

His skin was hot under her fingers as they trailed over his back, and he was breathing heavily again. She reached down and stroked the hard ridge hidden behind the falls of his trousers. "Do you like that?"

He sucked in a quick breath, then grinned. "Yes."

She did it again and he captured her mouth, his stroking tongue echoing the motion of her hand. "Perhaps," he said against her lips, "we should move to the bed."

"Mmhmm," she said, kissing him again as he walked them toward the big bed.

He lifted her up onto it, sliding the hem of her shift up as she settled onto the counterpane. His hands followed the hem and she shivered when his thumbs skimmed her bare breasts. Her shift went up over her head, then took its place on the floor, followed swiftly by her shoes and stockings.

She sat there naked on his bed, that small voice in the back of her mind warning her again about how ashamed she should feel. But she didn't feel ashamed, she felt hot and excited and ready.

"Touch me, Rhuddlan," she said breathlessly.

"Where?"

"Everywhere."

He obliged, palming her cheeks and leaning in for another kiss. His hands slid down her neck and shoulders, cupping her breasts again and giving them a slight squeeze.

"Ahhh," she gasped. A slight sense of frustration filled her when his hands continued to travel down her body, but it was quickly forgotten when his mouth replaced his hand and he sucked on her breast. Her head dropped back and her fingers slid into his hair. "Mmmm..."

He placed his body between her legs and laid her back onto the bed, pressing himself where she wanted him most. He licked and sucked for a moment longer, then began again on her other breast. She spread her legs wider, then locked her ankles at the small of his back.

"I want..."

When she didn't finish her thought, he gave her breast one last suck and met her eyes. "You want what?"

"I want to move," she said, lifting her hips. "I want you to press harder."

He obliged, rocking his own hips slowly as she began to move hers. "Yes," she breathed. "Like that."

"Do you want me to kiss you?" he asked, smoothing her hair back from her face.

"Yes," she said again, "my mouth and my breasts."

He obeyed, capturing her lips once, twice, then running his tongue over her nipple before drawing it into his mouth. "Like that?" he asked, his mouth still against her body.

Her hands slipped to his shoulders, her fingertips digging into his skin as her hips picked up speed. "Like that," she confirmed, as a familiar sensation began to build. "Oh God, like that."

He followed her lead and rocked faster, giving her what she needed. Her eyes closed and her head went back again, thrusting her breasts in the air as he moved from one to the other.

She couldn't remember the last time she'd felt this good.

The sensation broke over her and she sucked in a breath, clutching his shoulders. "Rhudd– Rhuddlan... Yes..."

He ground against her for a few more strokes before her whole body went limp, satisfied. "Oh, Rhuddlan..."

She opened her eyes to find him staring at her, his mouth rapidly curving into a smile. "My God, Olivia." He bent down and kissed her once more, one hand sliding down to grasp her backside. "That was..."

"Good," she said, trying to catch her breath. "Very good."

"And we're only getting started." He left her for a moment to draw back the bedclothes, then lifted her and placed her on the cool sheets. "Are you ready for more?"

"I will be in a minute," she said, grinning. "You?"

He unbuttoned the falls of his trousers, letting his member spring free. Her eyes must have widened because he looked down and chuckled. "It will fit. I promise."

That made her laugh. "Oh, I know it will fit. I was just appreciating your form."

"Oh."

"Are you disappointed?"

He shucked his trousers and climbed onto the bed and got under the sheet with her. "Disappointed?"

"That I'm not a virgin," she clarified, sucking in a breath when his hand slid down over her belly without warning.

"No," he replied firmly as his hand cupped her hip. "I don't need to be your first. I just want to be your best."

His hand dipped between her thighs, his thumb grazing her nub, and her head lolled back against the pillow. "You're doing rather well on that front," she said. "What can I do for you?"

He looked surprised by the question, even though she'd already mentioned wanting to do her share of the pleasuring. Had he not heard that in bed before?

After a moment he sat up, piling pillows behind him. "Straddle me," he said, stretching his legs out, "with your back to me."

She'd never been asked to do that before but complied, interested to see how this would play out.

"You'll want to be on your knees."

"All right." She got herself up on her knees, hovering over the tip of his manhood, and she could see what he was thinking. "Are you ready?"

She felt his lips on her back, his hands on her hips, and need began to course through her body once again.

"Very," he murmured against her skin and she lowered herself down, taking him slowly inside her.

His hands slid up her body as she sunk down onto him, cupping her plump breasts and giving them a gentle squeeze. "Oh, Livie," he groaned.

She tipped her head back, resting it on his shoulder as her breath began to quicken again. "I like this..."

"You're in control," he said softly in her ear. "You decide how fast or slow, how deep you take me."

She rose up so that only the last inch of him was still in contact with her body, then relaxed her legs and took him all the way back in. A half-tortured, half-approving sound rumbled in his chest so she did it again, then again. Her own arousal grew and she moved a little faster, covering his large hands on her breasts with her smaller ones, holding them against her.

"Like that?" she asked, though his heavy breathing answered the question for her.

She squeezed her inner muscles and he moaned. "Like...that..."

One of his hands left her breast and found its way between her thighs, stroking her slick nub and sending a bolt of pleasure through her body. "Lucas," she panted. "Yes..." His hips moved with hers, his hand still working her nub, and her climax began to build. "I'm... close..."

She moved faster, squeezing her inner muscles on every upstroke, the pleasure building inside her driving her on. When he kneaded her breast again, it sent her over the edge and she cried out. He stroked inside her a few more times, then pulled out and finished himself off with his own hand between her legs.

He collapsed back onto the pillows he'd piled up and she laid on his chest, drained but sated.

"I didn't know it could be like that," she said, reaching back to run a hand over his cheek and trying to catch her breath.

He kissed her neck, then her shoulder, wrapping one arm around her. "Didn't I promise you pleasure?"

She laughed a little. "Yes you did. And once again, you've kept your promise."

"I always will," he murmured, shifting beneath her to press a kiss to her temple. "Always."

She slid her fingers through his damp hair, answering softly. "I know."

Chapter Eleven

RHUDDLAN ROSE WITH the sun the next morning, despite sleeping little the night before. He'd awoken several times in the night, spending long, peaceful moments with Olivia in his arms or lying in hers before drifting off to sleep once more. But he'd sent instructions to the company of men escorting Nick back from Deganwy, asking them to meet him in an abandoned barn a few miles away from Rhuddlan Hall, and he needed to be on his way early.

He didn't want his brother anywhere near Olivia or any of his other dependents, but he needed to look the man in the eye one more time. Could he really prosecute his own brother, knowing what a guilty verdict would mean? Or was it enough to send him to some forlorn place where he could live out the rest of his days with only a jailor for company?

The morning sky was overcast, the wind blowing cold in a preview of the chilly autumn weather to come, but it suited Rhuddlan's mood as he rode out of the stable on Hermes. Whatever he chose as Nick's fate, this day also meant that saying goodbye to Olivia was nigh. That hurt as much as losing his brother, if in a different way, for he was losing the woman he was now certain he loved. She'd been the one bright spot in his life these past weeks, but he knew her stay at Rhuddlan Hall was always meant to be temporary. He scowled at the sky, wondering if he had the strength to do what was needed this day.

When Rhuddlan arrived at the barn, he found Nick's escort already there.

"How was the ride from Deganwy?" he asked Ellis, the company's man in charge, outside the old barn.

"Longer than I expected, Your Grace," Ellis returned. "He wouldn't come quietly, so we were obliged to restrain him. Thought it would be better if prying eyes didn't see him riding pillion behind one of my men, all tied up, so we had to hire a carriage to transport him."

Rhuddlan frowned, unhappy but unsurprised. "Where is he now?"

"Inside with two of my men."

"I'll see him alone for a moment, then I'll have instructions for the next leg of your journey."

Ellis nodded and gave a short bow before showing Rhuddlan to the barn entrance. Only one door was open, throwing a rectangle of dim sunlight onto the floor. Nick sat further back in a pile of old straw, his hands and feet bound with stout rope, his dark hair disheveled, and a smudge of dirt on his face.

One of Ellis's men stood guard on either side of him, and Rhuddlan dismissed them.

"Come to gloat, brother?" Nick asked flatly when his escorts had gone outside.

"Not to gloat, Nicu," Rhuddlan said. His voice was quiet but firm. "To decide what to do with you."

"Am I not to be put through a sham of a trial and hanged?" Nick asked, one eyebrow arching in question.

Rhuddlan ignored the dig at the court's integrity. "A trial is one possibility. The other is exile."

"Well, that worked well for Napoleon," Nick quipped.

"The first time, perhaps," Rhuddlan returned more sharply than he'd intended. "But you won't be ruling Elba with your own personal regiment on hand for protection." He took a breath, then tried again. "You left four innocent people to the mercy of monsters and tried to kill me. And that was just your final act. Are you at all sorry for what you did?"

"Only that I didn't complete my task," Nick said, his voice emotionless once more.

The final nail in Nick's metaphorical coffin, then. He'd all but admitted that, given even the tiniest opportunity, he'd come after Rhuddlan—and perhaps those he was close to—again.

"Then I have a question for you, likely the last choice you'll ever make," Rhuddlan said evenly, hoping he was making the right decision. Nick's brows rose, and Rhuddlan continued, "The York or the Retribution?"

"What?"

"Which prison hulk would you like to be housed on?"

Nick, predictably, scoffed. "Those are for criminals and prisoners of war, and they're temporary lodging at that."

Rhuddlan nodded. "Usually, yes. But, with a little help from a friend, I can get you lifetime accommodations aboard either the HMS York or the HMS Retribution. The York is newly converted, but I expect it to have similar conditions to the others of its class by the time you arrive."

Nick blanched. He'd heard the same stories Rhuddlan had about the prison hulks being crowded and filthy, with dreadful food and no quarantine for sick inmates. Either ship would be a dark, disgusting place to live with little hope of escape.

"Why don't you just kill me?" he asked, marshalling what appeared to be the last of his defiance. "Why not take me to trial and let me be executed?"

"Because the prison hulk is what you deserve."

Rhuddlan turned, nodding to the men to close the door behind him as he left the barn. "You'll bed down here tonight," he said to Ellis when he reached the yard once again. "Tomorrow you'll set off for the Isle of Sheppey. See your usual contact in London when you arrive there for more detailed instructions."

"Yes, Your Grace."

"There's a bonus for you and your men if you get your cargo to his final destination."

Ellis grinned. "I always get them there, Your Grace."

Rhuddlan acknowledged the truth of that statement with a nod. "Be especially careful with this one."

He strode over to Hermes and mounted the horse, glancing once more at the barn that held his baby brother. Rhuddlan knew he'd likely feel guilty for deciding on this punishment, particularly if an inmate came aboard with some deadly, contagious disease. But after the destruction of property and lives Nick had orchestrated, he truly did deserve to live out his days in a hellhole. And if his conscience prodded him about it,

Rhuddlan swore he'd simply recall the picture of his brother standing over him with that fowling piece, ready to kill him.

He rode Hermes hard, much to the delight of the stallion, and took the long way back to Rhuddlan Hall. When he arrived, Olivia was sitting in the drawing room embroidering.

She looked up from her work when he opened the door and smiled shyly. "I found your note this morning."

The memory of writing her a note while she lay in his bed sleeping naked replaced his troubles with Nick momentarily, and he smiled in return. "I would rather have been there myself when you woke."

She stood, placing the material she'd been sewing on her chair. "As would I. But such a beautiful note was the next best thing."

She walked toward him, and he met her halfway across the room, wrapping her in his arms and kissing her softly, wishing he smelled like something sweeter than horse and sweat. "I'm glad it sufficed."

Her arms came around him, her fingers threading through his hair. "And the business you saw to this morning?"

"It's done," he said, palming her cheek. "You're safe now."

"Lord Nicholas?"

"Will spend the rest of his long life wishing for death," Rhuddlan answered without preamble. "He's bound for a prison hulk moored on the other side of England."

The tension in her body flooded out, and he felt her relax against him. "That's a good compromise between hanging and transportation."

"I thought so, too." He placed a kiss on her temple, whispering, "And now you can have your life back."

They held each other without speaking for what felt like seconds and hours all at the same time. Then she drew back and kissed his lips, smiling. "Thank you, Lucas," she murmured. "Though it won't be my old life I go back to, will it?"

"No, I suppose not," he replied, resting his forehead against hers. "A new home, with no more worries about income or cruel men or blackmail."

"I still have my mother's debts to pay," she reminded him.

"No you don't."

"Yes, I—" She pulled away a little to look him in the eye. "Did you?"

He nodded. "One less thing for you to worry about."

"Rhuddlan..."

He bent his head and captured her lips briefly. "What happened to Lucas?" he asked with a smile.

"Is that what you prefer?" A blush began to creep up her neck and into her cheeks, and he knew she was remembering the last time she used his Christian name.

"It is since last night," he said quietly. "For as long as I live, I will never forget how you sounded when you called my name in bed."

Her forehead met his shoulder, but she was grinning. "Then Lucas it will be, when we are private together."

He kissed her hair, then asked the next inevitable question. "Will we be private together again?"

She looked up at him, her blue eyes unreadable. "You did promise to call on me once I'm settled in the new house. We will certainly be alone there."

"Except for Artie," he said lightly.

"Except for Artie," she chuckled. "Though we can always shut the door."

"Is that what you want?" he asked, unsure of which answer he wanted her to give. "To be my mistress?"

Seconds after the words left his mouth he regretted them. No honorable gentleman would ever say such a thing to a respectable lady. But Olivia didn't seem offended by the question.

"I'm honestly not sure," she said, her brow wrinkling as the conflict played out on her face. "I think I love you, Lucas. And what we had last night, what we did... It was wonderful."

She thought she loved him? His brain seized on that phrase and tried to call a halt to all other operations, but he forced himself to pay attention to the rest of her words.

"But I need to be on my own, at least for a while. I need to learn how to live without fear, and to take care of myself again. I cannot go directly from being under your literal protection to being your paramour—"

He opened his mouth to speak, but she laid a finger over his lips.

"—or anything else. I need to not be dependent upon anyone to truly have my life back."

His mind could understand the logic of her words— he would feel the same way had their positions been reversed—but his heart felt as though it had been stomped on. "Of course," he managed. "That was always the plan, wasn't it?"

"Falling in love with you was never part of the plan," she replied softly. "And I can't make you any promises about the future. That's what makes this so difficult."

"The feeling is mutual, darling," he said, swallowing down the urge to make love to her until she changed her mind. Even if he succeeded and she stayed, she would eventually grow discontented, chaffing at the bond that held her there rather than cherishing it. "Rhuddlan Hall is your home for as long as you like. It—and I—will always be here for you."

She tightened her arms around him. "It's probably best if I go today."

He nodded. "Shall we say our goodbyes now, while we are private?"

"Yes," she breathed, pulling him down to her for gentle, deep kiss.

He broke away for a moment to lock the drawing room door, then took her hand and led her to the sofa. Sliding his hands into her hair, he kissed her again, nipping at her lips, dropping kisses down her neck. In one motion they moved onto the sofa, Olivia's knees on either side of Rhuddlan's hips. He unbuttoned the top few buttons of her gown, sliding her bodice down as she worked the buttons on the falls of his trousers.

"Tell me what you want," he said, his breathing rapid.

"I want you inside me," she whispered. She opened the last button and pulled his member free, rubbing the tip at her entrance. They groaned simultaneously when she took him slowly in, settling in his lap for a moment to pull her arms from the sleeves of her gown. He lifted her breasts from beneath her stays and shift, sucking first one nipple then the other into his mouth.

"Lucas," she breathed, drawing out his name as if she wanted it to last on her lips.

"Livie," he murmured as she lifted herself up, hands braced on his shoulders, then slowly relaxed against him. She did it again, already beginning to pick up speed, and his head lolled back against the sofa.

She leaned forward, pressing her breasts against his chest and he regretted not shedding his tailcoat when he'd had the chance. But her eyes closed and she moaned, and he instantly changed his mind.

"Do you like that?" he asked.

She nodded and he moved his hands to her legs, sliding them up her stockings to the bare skin he sought. She clenched her inner muscles around him and he squeezed her hips.

"Do you like that?" she asked with a grin.

"Yes," he said, the word hissed as much as spoken. "Livie, yes..."

He slid one hand to her cleft and thumbed her nub, gratified when her back arched, pushing her breasts more firmly against him. Her movements became uncoordinated, and he knew she was close. He flexed his hips, stroking inside her when she became unable to continue the rhythm on her own.

"Lucas..."

His thumb brushed her nub again, exerting a little more pressure and rubbing in time with his stroking, and she gasped, climaxing in his arms. The ecstasy was plain on her beautiful face, his name on her lips, and he had to concentrate to keep from coming with her.

He waited until her peak had passed, then pulled his member from her body and finished himself off against her naked thigh. It was messier, which he would regret in a few minutes, but he didn't want to take the chance of getting her with child. Her life had been decided for her once before; he didn't want to put her in that position again.

She slumped against him, pressing her lips to his jaw. "I love you, Lucas Blake," she whispered in his ear.

"I love you, Olivia Stone," he answered softly, purposely using her alias. He hadn't known Olivia Lockwood, the daughter of a wealthy merchant betrothed to an earl's heir. But Olivia Stone, seamstress and dog owner, had captured his heart.

It took Olivia three weeks in her new house to stop jumping at every little sound, four before she could walk with Artie around the grounds without looking over her shoulder every few minutes. By the beginning of the sixth week she realized she was sleeping all the way through the night again, no longer waking in a cold sweat and wondering how best to flee without being seen.

Artie helped her begin to feel safe again, of course, simply by being a large, ferocious looking dog, but also by becoming her protector more than ever before. He took it upon himself to inspect rooms when she walked into them, to investigate sounds, to periodically sniff the air and ground, to be alert and on guard so she didn't always have to be. If Artie was relaxed, Olivia knew she could relax, and they spent many comfortable evenings before the fire in the Marquess of Hadley's former study.

One thing she never quite got used to, though, was the almost complete absence of Rhuddlan's presence in her life. He kept his distance as she'd requested, save the letters they exchanged. It started as a note Olivia sent with Mrs. Andersen on market day, asking her to detour to Rhuddlan Hall on her way to the village about a week after Olivia had relocated to the new house. She'd wanted to let him know that she was settling in and that she adored the house. She'd also wanted badly to tell him how much she missed him, but thought better of it after their rather emotional parting.

He'd sent a note back the following day with one of his stable lads, asking after her physical comfort, her health, and Artie's welfare. The stable lad told her he was to wait for a reply but she hadn't known what to write under pressure. She sent the stable lad back with a message to pass along to Rhuddlan: thank you for the reply, we are both well, more to follow. She'd then composed a reply later, and sent it with Mrs. Andersen on her way to the village.

The letter exchange turned into something of a ritual, something she looked forward to every week. But it didn't make up for the feel of his hands on her body, the fun of playing cards with him, the comfort of lying in his arms, or any of the hundred things she'd come to love about him.

"Has His Grace come to call yet?" Mrs. D. asked during her own visit. She was sitting with Olivia and Miss H. in Olivia's drawing room while they worked from their respective sewing baskets.

"No," Olivia answered, shifting her gaze to the beams of autumn sun shining through her windows. "I've asked him not to yet."

"Yet?" Miss H. asked, eyebrows raised. "It's been over a month since you left him."

Left him. Well, that was what she had done. She'd packed her things and gone with no promises and no hope for the future. "I wanted to be on my own for a while."

"After what you went through, I don't blame you," Mrs. D. said. "It was nearly a year after Mr. Davies met his maker before I found myself wanting a companion, and his death was peaceful."

"What is that you're working on, Olivia?" Miss H. asked.

Olivia held up the red satin waistcoat she'd been embroidering. "What do you think?"

The two older women twittered over the quality of the fabric and the tiny dragons that roared across the garment at regular intervals.

"He'll wear it with pride, I'm sure," Miss H. said with a smile.

"I haven't even told you who it's for," Olivia protested, but it was a weak effort. Blood red and dragons meant only one person for her.

Mrs. D. patted Olivia's knee. "Perhaps it's time to invite him to call, eh?"

The women stayed another hour, then Olivia found herself walking with Artie to the dark-paneled study for a sheet of paper. "What shall I say to him, Loup Garou? Should I ask him to call, as Mrs. D. suggested? Or shall I simply tell him how much I miss him?"

She sat down at what had been Lord Hadley's desk and began to write, telling Rhuddlan how she was finally starting to feel like herself again, and yes, that she missed him. She extended an open invitation to come calling at his convenience and signed it "Livie."

When she appeared in the kitchen with the sealed letter in her hand, Mrs. Andersen smiled broadly. "Tomorrow isn't market day, Miss Lockwood."

"I know," Olivia replied. "You wouldn't happen to be going to the village anyway, would you?"

"No," the housekeeper said slyly. "But I could be going to Rhuddlan Hall if you wanted me to."

"It's not too much trouble?"

Mrs. Andersen shook her head. "If you're sending him a note on a different day this week, I'm guessing it's because it's important."

"I think it is," Olivia replied, handing over the letter. "We'll see if he does."

Two days went by with no word from Rhuddlan, and Olivia began to wonder if she'd missed her chance. While she was figuring out how to go on in this new life of hers, had he found clarity and a future that didn't include her? Had he begun looking for a woman who would stabilize his reputation and make an excellent duchess?

On the third day, a knock sounded at the front door. Mr. Andersen was outside chopping wood and Mrs. Andersen was baking bread in the kitchen, the smell permeating every room, so Olivia went to answer it herself.

"I'm not too late, am I Miss Stone?"

Rhuddlan stood there before her, his unbuttoned greatcoat swirling around him in the breeze, a hopefully expression on his face.

She was frozen for what felt like minutes but was likely only a few seconds. Then she managed a smile and gestured him inside. "Of course not, Your Grace."

He walked just a few steps into the house, then turned to her and took her hand. "I'm sorry for not coming sooner. My summons arrived for Parliament, and I must return to London in a few weeks. I've spent the last two days issuing orders and signing papers in preparation for the journey. This was the first moment I could get away."

Her smile widened, and she suspected the relief showed on her face. "I understand," she said, giving his hand a gentle squeeze. "Why don't we go and sit in the drawing room?"

Their eyes met when she said the words "drawing room," and she knew he was remembering the last time they'd been in such a place together. She was remembering it, too. She took a breath and held it for a moment, trying to calm her racing heart. "I'll order tea and we can talk."

She showed him to the drawing room, popping briefly into the kitchen to request a tea tray. When she returned to the drawing room, she found Rhuddlan standing by one window looking out over the grounds, his greatcoat draped over a nearby chair.

"It's a beautiful view this time of year, with the leaves turning colors," she said, coming up beside him.

He took her hand once again and brought it to his lips for a kiss. "I'm glad you like it. You seem at home here."

"I am," she said, realizing the truth of the statement. "And thanks to your generosity, I'm finding my way as lady of this little manor."

"I'm glad to see someone in this house who loves it as much as Hadley did," he said with a small smile.

"That's not exactly what I meant," she said, turning to take his other hand. "Your generosity in giving me this property was amazing, certainly. But I meant the generosity you showed when you let me go on my own terms. I know how hard it was for me to leave you behind, but I can only imagine how painful it was for you to watch me go with no guarantee we'd ever be together again."

He brought both her hands to his chest, and she could feel his heart beating almost as rapidly as her own.

"It was the hardest thing I ever did," he confessed. "But you said you loved me, and I trusted you with my heart. When your note came this week and it was signed 'Livie'..." He paused for what sounded like his own calming breath. "I knew I'd done the right thing. You are the family I've chosen, Livie. You're the person I trust most in the world."

Her heart took off at a gallop and those blasted tears came to her eyes. Why was she crying when she'd never felt happier? She took one of her hands back to swipe at her eyes, then laughed, giving it back to him. "I don't know what's come over me."

"Adoration for your betrothed, perhaps?"

"But we're not— We can't— Lucas, I can't be a duchess," she said, finally getting a whole thought out. "My mother's debts might be paid, but I am still a ruined woman."

"If Devonshire can live with his wife and mistress in the same house at the same time and not suffer for it, I can marry a woman who was forced into the arms of a footman," he replied, planting a kiss on each of her hands. "That is, if you will make me the happiest of men." He arched a dark eyebrow at her and laughed a little. "But you already do. Livie, please just say you'll marry me so I can stop talking and kiss you."

"Yes!" She released his hands and threw her arms around him. Her eyes closed when his arms wrapped around her, and his warm lips found hers. When they parted, she blurted out, "I will likely be a disaster of a duchess, my love, but if it means being with you for the rest of our lives, I'll do it."

The drawing room door flew open and Artie came racing into the room, barking at the sight of a newcomer until he got close enough to sniff.

"There's the Loup Garou," Rhuddlan grinned, reaching down to scratch the dog's ears. "You're cold, pup. Have you been outside?"

Mr. Andersen appeared a moment later followed by his wife with the tea tray, blushing and apologizing for the interruption. "I took him for a walk, Miss

Lockwood, but he got away from me once we got back to the house."

"He knew someone else was here today," Olivia said with a laugh. Then an idea struck her. "Would you mind taking him out again, Mr. Andersen? I think he needs to run around a bit more yet."

"Of course," Mr. Andersen replied, glancing at Mrs. Andersen. "Come on ye old dog, let's let your mistress have her privacy."

When he and Mrs. Andersen had taken Artie out and shut the door firmly behind them, Olivia turned back to Rhuddlan, ignoring the tea tray and tracing a finger down the edge of his waistcoat. "I have a gift for you," she said with a slow smile.

"You do?"

"Mmhmm. It's a waistcoat in Rhuddlan colors. Would you like to see it?"

His mouth spread into a matching smile at the seductive tone in her voice.

"It's in my bedchamber. And you'll have to try it on to be sure of the fit."

He pulled her closer, cupping her derriere with both hands. "You'll help me remove my current clothing, won't you?"

"If you trust me to do so," she murmured, brushing her lips over his.

"I will always trust you to disrobe me, Livie my love," he chuckled. Then he became serious, sliding his hands up her back. "And to handle my heart gently."

"I promise to do both," she said, smiling, "with equal measures of care."

"I love you," he said softly, dipping his head to capture her mouth with his.

"And I love you," she replied. "Always."

Author's Note

When we first started planning this series, I made a joke about using Vlad Dracula as my legend. I'd been having a hard time coming up with a figure who could be adapted to a Georgian- or Regency-set story, and on the surface, Vlad is about as far away from a romantic hero as a person can get. But I've always been rather contrary, and once I'd articulated the idea of transforming the Impaler Prince into a swoon-worthy fictional character, I started wondering if it could actually be done.

As it turns out, Vlad was not really the man legend has made him out to be. By modern standards he was most certainly cruel, and he really did use impalement as his preferred method of punishment. But what most people don't realize is that he was a man of his time and place. He spent his childhood at a hostile court as a hostage to ensure his father's compliance. He had to fight—literally—to become ruler of Wallachia, and was dethroned twice. He wasn't the only, or even the first, ruler to impale his enemies. Stephen III of Moldavia, for example, was at least as enthusiastic about employing the stake as his neighbor in Wallachia, and he was later sainted by the Orthodox Church.

He also received what I've been calling the Richard III treatment, where history and literature have made him out to be a rather different man than his contemporaries probably knew. Where Shakespeare characterized Richard III as a murderous, hunchbacked villain, the Transylvanian Saxons spread rumors, some based in truth, some unverifiable, that Vlad III Dracula was the devil of Wallachia. The use of the brand new printing press and the public's love of gothic tales, helped spread the Saxons pamphlets similarly to theater companies performing Shakespeare's plays. A fellow named Bram Stoker may have added a bit more to the public's opinion of Vlad, as well.

For this book, I adapted the basic outline of Vlad's adult life: he was deposed as Prince of Wallachia, then became a fugitive and the commander of a rebel army before restoring himself to the throne. At the beginning of Rhuddlan's story, he is the ruling prince as it were, then he goes on the run to Liverpool with Olivia before the final showdown with his brother. Lord Nicholas, too, is loosely based on Vlad's brother, Radu the Handsome, who deposed his brother as Prince of Wallachia with the help of Sultan Mehmed II (played here by the Duke of Cumberland).

The personalities of historical figures are often difficult to discern, and these characters are no different. As Vlad was a man of his time and one to whom history has not been kind, so too was Rhuddlan. I also gave him a bit of a Hades aesthetic to round him out—a man who took his job very seriously, who was responsible for (in Rhuddlan's case) thousands of souls and who carries that weight with him always. It's always why he makes a joke about Artie being Cerberus in disguise. Olivia was not meant to be the embodiment of Persephone, but she did get a little of Pers's aesthetic as well. Rhuddlan calls her the light of his life and compares himself to the darkness in the world. And Olivia got to be a badass when she needed to be, but was still her feminine, fabric-loving self.

There are lots of other historical tidbits sprinkled throughout the story, too. You can visit the Pinterest board (https://www.pinterest.com/coralee49/boards/) I made for this book and check them out.

If you're interested in reading more about Vlad III Dracula, my two favorite books were Radu Florescu's *Dracula, Prince of Many Faces: His Life and His Times* (nonfiction) and C.C. Humphreys's *Vlad: The Last Confession* (fiction).

A Legend To Love Series

Chapter 1 Excerpt from

His Duchess At Eventide
A Legend To Love

Chapter One

November 1805

WIND WHIPPED CAPTAIN Lord Cheverley's improvised sail against his raft's mast. Salted sea-spray stung his lips and gusts roared in his ears. Using his shoulder, he wiped rain from his eyes and then re-wedged the paddle between his left arm and leg. Thighs straining, he gripped the groaning rudder.

He hadn't survived the unspeakable—seven years of war, a shipwreck, the loss of his right arm below the elbow, and six excruciating years of captivity—only to fail now.

Had he?

Wine-dark depths did not defer to long-serving officers of the Royal Navy. Frothy white waves were indifferent to sons of dukes. And life-hungry storms didn't give a damn if they stripped wives of their husbands, or sons of their fathers.

Penelope. Thaddeus. Vast emptiness yawned. Instinctively, he beseeched the heavens. Please. I must survive.

No god answered, only darkness without direction, no land, no guiding stars. The blank, shifting water beneath promised death—the same, slow demise that had claimed the lives of Chev's fellow seamen stationed with him on the HMS Defiance.

That gale, too, had materialized as if summoned by Poseidon's trident, without warning and yet powerful enough to devour his sixty-four-gun ship. Rocks like rusted knives protruded from a deadly shoal. Waves thundered without reprieve, breaking the Defiance into pieces unfit for kindling. And his ship's end had been only the beginning of his nightmare.

Tu n'es rien. You are nothing. Je possède chaque partie de tu, maintenant. I own every part of you, now.

His raft listed. He spit over the side.

How much adversity could a man face before he surrendered to annihilation's mercy? How god-damned much?

The wind bellowed. Siren whispers sounded, sensing weakness—supplicate, surrender, submit.

What did he have to offer the world he'd left behind? He'd thought he'd return a hero. Instead, he was broken in body and soul. If he yielded to the storm, would it not be kinder to his family and a just restitution for his sins?

Memories feathered through his thoughts. His face buried in the softness of Penelope's hair. Her fingers, drifting in soothing circles against the small of his back.

He inhaled deep, straining against invisible bonds and roaring back into the wind. He cursed fate. He cursed God. He cursed the pirate witch who'd kept him captive. Then, he cursed himself.

His anger crystalized in breath, clouding the chilled air. He'd escaped captivity, darkness, restraints. Zephyr's winds and Poseidon's waves demanded the final say, but he would not give up without a fight.

Not tonight.

The bundle strapped across his back held what little remained of hung beef and brandy. His cask of fresh water ran low, but he had enough to last another day.

He smothered his weakness, gritted his teeth, and held fast to the rudder.

He'd survive.

He'd survive on the pure need for vengeance.

For years, while Penelope labored to transform her husband's estate, Pensteague House, into a haven, she'd done her best to ignore the specter of neighboring Ithwick Manor, her husband's birthplace. At her worst, she'd wished the house and grounds would simply wither away. Then, however, the duke had been hale, his heir, Piers, alive, and she and her son superfluous to the duchy.

Now, everything had changed, and light filtering through the ducal library's windows chastised her for those fancies—the carpets were worn, the centuries-old relics, dust-laden, and a must-heavy scent burned inside the bridge of her nose. Hour by listless hour, time had been devouring what was left of her husband's boyhood world. And Ithwick's slow demise provided none of her hoped-for triumph.

Still, having done her duty, called on the duke, and reported on Thaddeus's education and care—not that His Grace had appeared to understand a word—she itched to leave this place full of ghosts and greed, mother to the heir or not.

Mrs. Renton—the duke's devoted housekeeper, and one of the few Ithwick residents Penelope trusted—wrung her liver-spotted hands.

"You must stay here at Ithwick," Mrs. Renton said, her pale eyes wide. "The duchy is without a duchess. The duke has lost his sense. Thaddeus remains too young to assume an heir's duties, and I am certain those...those..." Mrs. Renton gestured to the window, "...men mean to destroy everything that's left!"

Moving to the window, Penelope's gaze found the duke's closest male relatives apart from her son. The elder was Mr. Anthony, who, as a descendant of the last duke's brother, was next in line to inherit after Penelope's son. The younger was a more recent arrival, the duke's sister's son, Lord Thomas.

Absurd for those gentlemen and their friends to be littered about the lawn in winter, despite the unusually warm weather. Ridiculous, too, to be having a weighted disc throwing competition while attired in the latest, highly impractical fashion.

Penelope touched one of the pins in her tightly knotted hair and then rested her hand against the neckline of her outdated muslin. Unexpected discomfort blossomed in her chest. Hot, outsized discomfort.

Had Mr. Anthony, Lord Thomas, and their friends no shame? Even now, beyond the restless channel, young men were sacrificing their lives defending these craggy shores in a war that had already cost Penelope her husband.

"It appears to me"—Penelope's voice tinged with bitterness—"Mr. Anthony and Lord Thomas's only aspiration is a perpetual, decadent house party."

"It is worse than decadence! It is unnatural ambition."

Unnatural ambition? Pen knew them to be irresponsible, certainly, but to accuse them of intentionally usurping the duchy's power?

"Don't you see?" Mrs. Renton asked. "Mr. Anthony brought suit to have your husband declared dead—you need look no further for evidence."

Penelope turned. "Mr. Anthony claimed the suit was necessary in order to free funds for Thaddeus." That was, however, before they'd discovered the surprise codicil to Cheverley's will granting Penelope full possession of Pensteague.

"Mr. Anthony," Mrs. Renton replied, "also claims His Grace is in complete accord with every decision he makes. But, you've seen for yourself—His Grace's words are unintelligible. As for Lord Thomas, he often returns late"—Mrs. Renton lowered her voice —"smelling of tipple and perfume."

Penelope frowned. The amorous exploits of her husband's cousin weren't any of her concern.

On the other hand, she could not deny His Grace's troubling condition. The duke's blank stare had sent shivers through her spine. For the first time, she'd felt a measure of compassion toward the tyrant.

But compassion for the duke and a willingness to intercede on his behalf were two very different positions.

"If those actions weren't awful enough," Mrs. Renton continued, "several women have left our employ so distressed they did not request references. The remaining women serve as mistresses and little else."

Penelope's flush spread to her cheeks. A man had to be vile-hearted to take advantage of anyone in their employ in such a way. "If you would, Mrs. Renton, supply the names and direction of those who left. I will provide references for them from Pensteague."

"Thank you, Lady Cheverley." Mrs. Renton bobbed a short curtsey. "But what of Mr. Anthony and Lord Thomas?"

Penelope gazed back out to the lawn. Were they merely reckless libertines as she'd long assumed, or were they greedy, dangerous men emboldened by the duke's illness, Thaddeus's youth, and his mother's perceived lack of connections?

Anthony had come to Ithwick following the duke's sudden illness and—at Piers's request—had taken over the duties of steward. After Pier's death, Lord Thomas had arrived. They'd been indifferent to Penelope and only cursorily interested in Thaddeus, and she was happy enough to allow things to remain as they were.

But what if they were intentionally robbing Ithwick? What remedy could she bring? She'd need solicitors, barristers, and witnesses to bring suit.

Though Pensteague thrived, she returned every sixpence earned to the estate...the only way she could care for the wounded seamen who regularly appeared on Pensteague's doorstep.

She'd taken the land her husband, Cheverley, had been granted as part of his mother's marriage settlement—a small cottage with surrounding forests and wastes—and transformed it into a thriving estate with choice livestock, crops, fallows, and coppiced wood. She'd raised Thaddeus without assistance from his ducal grandparents. She'd remained dutiful and loyal to Cheverley—and, by extension the duchy—all while striving to provide the wounded seamen Pensteague sheltered the dignity of a generous livelihood. And now, Pensteague was hers and hers alone.

Why should she place all she protected and all she'd built at risk?

"Mrs. Renton," she began, "you've always shown me kindness—"

"You were devoted to young Lord Cheverley," Mrs. Renton interrupted, sniffling. "I had hoped—"

"Allow me to speak plain." Penelope's own dashed hopes were difficult enough to bear, thank you. "To Lord Cheverley's family—everyone but the late duchess —I have always been an interloper. It is not my place to interfere."

"But there is no one else," Mrs. Renton replied. "Mr. Anthony acts as if he is master of Ithwick. You are the only one who can stop him."

"Mr. Anthony has been inclined to be pompous for as long as I have known him." But pompous and criminal did not negate one another, did they?

Pen attempted to rationalize again. "Isn't it natural Mr. Anthony take an interest in running the estate? He is, after Thaddeus, the next in line to inherit."

"Mr. Anthony and his coterie are draining the coffers. They are depleting the livestock. Their mismanagement is so severe, long-time tenants are choosing not to renew their leases. Please help us, Lady Cheverley. If you do not protect Ithwick, I fear there will be nothing left for young Thaddeus to inherit." Mrs. Renton paced the length of the rug, paused, then glanced up at a painting. "If Lord Cheverley were here now, it's what he would wish you to do."

Pen's lips flattened at the invocation of her husband's name. Reluctantly, she turned her gaze to the painting she'd avoided since entering the room—a portrait of Cheverley and his older brother as boys.

Though in the portrait, Cheverley's pale blonde hair had yet to darken, his stance already hinted at future swagger. His sheepish half-smile acknowledged worlds he had yet to understand, let alone conquer, but his pale blue eyes alit with a sickle-sharp cunning and an insatiable thirst for adventure.

A thirst that would rob her of a husband and Thaddeus of a father.

Tears pricked the corners of her eyes. Foolish, foolish man.

She did not, however, regret their brief affair and whirlwind marriage. The experience had been transformative and grand—to the extent her sixteen-year-old mind could comprehend grand—a rush that had taken her from the threshold of womanhood to the full blossom of her feminine power. And what followed, though unpleasant, had been the gauntlet that formed her character.

She sighed.

Thirteen years had passed since she'd seen her husband, six since he disappeared off the coast of France, though she hadn't known the gut-wrenching details of his final hours until the recent trial to prove his death.

Cheverley's ship had left the Channel Fleet on orders to capture a French privateer. Soon after the privateer was won, Chev ordered his first mate to sail home the prize. Then, a sudden storm parted the ships, pushing the HMS Defiance off her reckoning by three degrees. But three mere degrees had altered the ship's course enough for the naval gunner to meet a gruesome, rocky end.

In the horrible hours it took the hull to break to pieces, Chev sent part of his crew in a cutter, hopeful they'd find harbor. He remained with his ship...exactly what Penelope would expect of her husband—always certain he could find or forge a way, always driven to display mythic heroism, even at the expense of those he held dear.

In this case, Chev failed. The cutter capsized. The few survivors drifted for days before being rescued. As for Cheverley...after reviewing the evidence, a judge declared him dead. No man, he said, could have survived the wreck.

Then again, her husband had not been just any man.

A burst of low, male laughter rose up from the lawn.

"They laugh while they drain the duchy dry," Mrs. Renton murmured. "They wouldn't have dared to set foot in the house in the first place if...if..."

"...If Lord Cheverley were here," Pen finished quietly.

Yes, she was weary. Yes, she could not spare the expense.

But could she truly turn her back on this part of her husband's past, forever denying skeletons that were not so much in a cupboard as atop a neighboring hill?

"Perhaps," Mrs. Renton whispered, "Lord Cheverley will yet return."

Penelope's neck prickled.

If she were honest, on nights when the moon's glow brightened the sheets of her marriage bed, loneliness pierced her heart like one of her husband's hand-crafted arrows, and she sometimes allowed herself to imagine Cheverley would return. ...

"Mrs. Renton"—she squelched irrational hope—"we must be careful what we wish. If Cheverley survived, a terrible fate must have befallen him. If he is alive, he is suffering."

She turned away from the portrait.

What would Chev have wanted her to do? If he were here, he would have wanted her to remain tucked up in the proper little jewel casing he'd prepared while he forged forth to set everything to rights in a spectacular show.

But he wasn't here. He hadn't been here for thirteen years.

The better question was—what did she wish to do? How much of what she'd built in Cheverley's name could she risk?

She turned about, taking in the ducal library and considering the stern faces of her husband's ancestors glaring down from centuries past.

If Mr. Anthony and Lord Thomas were corrupt, what would she be teaching Thaddeus if she remained ensconced in comfort while corruption flourished?

Corruption bred fear. Fear bred distrust, anger, divisions and even—if left unchecked—bloodshed.

She did have a responsibility, loath as she was to admit it. Whatever the cost now, it would pale in comparison to the future cost if these men succeeded in fully usurping the duchy's power. She must find a way to root out and remove the corruption. Not only for Thaddeus's sake, but for the sake of those, like Mrs. Renton, whose livelihoods depended on Ithwick.

"Mrs. Renton, I concede." Lord help her. "Thaddeus and I will take up residence at Ithwick, care for the duke and keep a close eye on Mr. Anthony and Lord Thomas. Having the heir and his mother present should gentle the worst of their conduct."

"And if they ask why?"

"I will tell them I intend to weave a shroud for Cheverley on the medieval loom upstairs."

"Bless you, my lady." Mrs. Renton's brows knit. "But is it wise to bring young Thaddeus? As Thaddeus's guardian, Lord Thomas could make trouble."

Let him try.

"Thaddeus goes where I go." In fact, Thaddeus was so protective, she couldn't have confined him to Pensteague if she wished. "Besides, both the duke and Lord Thomas serve as guardians. Thomas cannot assert himself without exposing the duke's state. And, in a few months, Thaddeus will be fourteen—old enough to choose his own guardians."

She recast her gaze toward the group of gentlemen below. Another drunken cheer rose from the lawn.

"You needn't worry any longer, Mrs. Renton." She spoke with bravado she did not feel. "I will become Ithwick's unlikely champion."

But were her adversaries indolent man-children, or were they a crawling nest of vipers?

And, if they were a nest of vipers—she chilled—which would be the first to sting?

*****End of excerpt His Duchess At Eventide (A Legend To Love series) by Wendy LaCapra*****

About the Author

A graduate of the University of Michigan with a major in history, Cora is the 2014 winner of the Royal Ascot contest for best unpublished Regency romance. She went on a twelve year expedition through the blackboard jungle as a high school math teacher before publishing *Save the Last Dance for Me*, the first book in the Maitland Maidens series.

When she's not walking Rotten Row at the fashionable hour or attending the entertainments of the Season, you might find her participating in Historical Novel Society and Romance Writers of America events, wading through her towering TBR pile, or eagerly awaiting the next Marvel movie release.

If you'd like to find out more about Cora or her books you can visit her online:

Website: http://coraleeauthor.wordpress.com

Newsletter: http://eepurl.com/bLwpm9

Facebook : http:/www.facebook.com/AuthorCoraLee

Goodreads: http:/www.goodreads.com/coralee49

Bookbub: https://www.bookbub.com/profile/cora-lee

Pinterest: https://www.pinterest.com/coralee49

Other Books By Cora Lee

Maitland Maidens series
Sweet Regency romance novellas to lighten your heart.

Save the Last Dance for Me
Mr. Benedict Grey is the only heir to a long-standing title, and he knows his duty: wed a suitable girl and secure the succession beyond himself. But if a gentleman could be called a wallflower, Benedict would fit the description perfectly. And for years he's been out of Society more than he's been in it. How will he find a woman to wed and bed when he can barely converse with the ladies of the *ton*?

Lady Honoria Maitland has promised her dying father that she would find a husband to take care of her. But she wants a gentleman that loves *her*, not her dowry or her name. When she reunites with her old friend Benedict, she proposes a faux betrothal. She can teach him how to woo a woman and simultaneously ease her father's last days. But Honoria's clever plan failed to account for Benedict's heart...or her own.

Back In My Arms Again
Mr. James Fitzsimmons is the son of a well-to-do farmer, solidly among the ranks of the gentry but not

privileged enough to move in the same circles as a duke's daughter. Meeting Lady Cecilia seventeen years ago was pure luck, but falling in love with her was pure torment. When she refused his offer of marriage he vowed to put her out of his mind—and his heart. But when James discovers a powerful lord is threatening to take the farm and ruin the Fitzsimmons name, he knows he needs an influential ally. Can James agree to Cecilia's terms and risk his heart once more to save his family?

Lady Cecilia Maitland has everything an unmarried woman could want: money of her own, high social status, and the ability to live life on her own terms. What she doesn't have is the only man she ever loved. She turned down James's proposal all those years ago and didn't see him again...until he turned up at a house party in search of a patron. Cecilia knows she can provide him the monetary and social support he needs if they marry, but will he accept such an offer from the woman who broke his heart? And what will it cost her if he does?

The Heart of a Hero series

What if superheroes were mortals who lived and loved during the Regency?

No Rest for the Wicked

Michael Devlin is a man of great learning but little means, living in one of the poorest sections of Dublin. By day, he practices law at the Four Courts and gives reading lessons to the local children. By night he's the man in the mask, prowling the streets of The Liberties defending the people—*his* people—from those who would prey upon them. But when his estranged wife appears on his doorstep with a summons from Sir Arthur Wellesley, both of Michael's worlds are turned upside down. What will happen to The Liberties if he obeys Sir Arthur's command to meet in Cork? Can he even trust the woman who married then left him five years ago?

As a spy for Sir Arthur Wellesley, Joanna Pearson Devlin has executed this same mission flawlessly many times before: locate the subject, transport him safely, and present him to her employer. When Sir Arthur sends her out one more time to bring in her estranged husband, Joanna knows *this* mission will be anything except flawless. But Napoleon's agents are everywhere, and Michael is an important part of the team Sir Arthur is assembling to stop them. For the sake of her country, Joanna heads to Dublin even as her discomfort grows. Will she be able to put aside her uncertainties and convince her husband to join the fight? Can they learn to work together again if he agrees?

The Good, The Bad, And The Scandalous
Andrew Elliott, Earl of Hartland, is no stranger to scandal. A notorious rake and eccentric genius, he fights crime in armor of his own design and celebrates his achievements with the merriest of widows. What the *ton* doesn't know is that Hart has received a warning: danger is heading for London and it's looking for Sarah Shipton.

Sarah discovers the bookshop her mother owns is failing and they will have nothing to live on when the month is out. So when the Earl of Hartland offers for her, she agrees to the marriage. But marrying Hart throws Sarah from the frying pan of imminent poverty into the fire of a world filled with science and peril she never knew existed.

How will Sarah cope with the knowledge that someone wants her dead? Can Hart keep her safe from a person hell bent on her destruction?